The Backbench Masti-Keers

I ♥ India

Boyz Rulz

notionpress.com

The Backbench Masti-Keers

Kumar Ravi

notionpress.com

Notion Press

Old No. 38, New No. 6

McNichols Road, Chetpet

Chennai - 600 031

First Published by Notion Press 2015

ISBN: 978-93-5206-284-3

Acknowledgement

Directly or indirectly, this venture was a special effort by so many people, who have affected, helped and inspired my life. As a denouement I emerged with the book – 'The Backbench Masti-keers'.

Thanks to the Backbenchers - Bhaskar, Sanjeet and Hitesh (Mrinal) who are the real characters in the novel.

My sincere Thanks to my parents, my wife, my friends, my well-wishers and God for his blessings, and for giving me such an ongoing colorful journey.

My special Thanks to my favorite teacher Mrs. Anita Dutt, who encouraged me to follow my passion and believe in myself and it inspires me always; my friends Ankit Bhaiya, Abhinav, Jasdeep, Manish, Niraj, Siva, Suman and Samir who helped and motivated me during the writing journey of The Backbench Masti-keers.

And, definitely thank you all for reading the book and relishing our fun-filled and dynamic journey!

Contents

Chapter One

Introducing the Backbenchers

"Wake up Sam! Wake up!"

"It's 8:30, man!" someone yelled.

My eyes finally opened. Reluctantly, I broke away from the dream I had. I saw the bright and beautiful rays of the sun that fell on my bed through the windows as the curtains blew in the light breeze. The cool morning freshness blended imperceptibly with the scent of deodorant which my roommate had used just before leaving. The cool and soothing environment compelled me to fall asleep again. But when I noticed the time, I woke up with a jolt as I recalled that we had S. Bose's class at 9:00 AM.

I was already thrown out of his class three times. He didn't allow late entries and unfortunately, we had most of his classes first thing in the morning. He was one of the martinets, but also one of the erudite professors in our college. Anyhow, I prepared myself physically and mentally for Wednesday's hectic schedule and ran to class like a superhero. While crossing the mess-quarters, I saw some students running down the stairs after eating a hasty breakfast, to reach class on time. Breakfast was one of the things which never interested me. I never liked to eat early in the morning.

When I saw one of my classmates running to class, I sped up and managed to catch him before he reached the classroom entrance. I lurked behind him while he was asking for permission to get in.

Finally, we were allowed to enter and I was relieved to find myself attending a class on Engineering Mechanics. I hastily stepped up to the last two rows and joined my friends. When I was about to reach my bench, a loud acerbic voice broke the silence. "You! What is your name?"

Everybody turned to look at me. It corroborated that his question was indeed for me. I turned around and found that Mr. Bose was staring at me with raised eyebrows. "Yes. You!" he said again.

"Sir, my name is Samar," I managed to speak bleakly.

"Are you aware of the rules in my class? I've been noticing you – you come to class late all the time. Is there a reason for it, my boy?" He seemed to have targeted me for everyone's amusement. With that, everybody's mood lightened up as there was expectation of some fun there. I was speechless. Last night, I was busy watching a pornographic movie on my roommate's newly bought laptop. I obviously could not say this in front of the whole class.

"Yes? I am asking you!" he said, pointedly looking at me.

Now I simply had to answer him. I made up a lame excuse of studying late into the night. He smiled at me gently. "Hmm. I see," he said, as though impressed by my answer. Almost immediately, he fired his next one. "Can you show me the assignment that I allotted yesterday?" Now I was in trouble.

"Sir, actually, I was absent yesterday. The topics were not clear to me. So, I was unable to do it," I said politely, to convince him. He looked at me confidently for a few seconds, as if he knew what to do next. Then, he took out the attendance register and started searching for something in it. I guessed that he was confirming my absence yesterday. But I was amazed when he addressed me again with his findings. "According to the attendance register, you were last present on the tenth, and that was Friday! I remember I took the second class on Force System Resultant." After a pause, he asked, "Can you show me that day's assignment?" Now nobody could have saved me. I was trapped completely.

"Beta! Teri to lag gayi! Ab nikal le yahan se!" a voice said in my head. I noticed that everybody in class was enjoying the entertainment in the morning. After all this, I realized that the next mandate for me would be to leave class. To avoid further humiliation I left the classroom saying, "Sorry sir!"

That was my fourth day of being marked absent in S. Bose's class. Though the event was embarrassing for me, I didn't let it hover over my mind. I stepped out on the corridor on my way to outside. After a few steps, I saw one of my studious classmates running to class. We called him 'Lui'. Yes, you got it right. He was christened with this name because of his physical appearance. A lanky physique, spectacles, a shabby look - it seemed like a vampire had sucked all his blood out of him. One could spot him from a hundred yards.

"Hey Moron! Where are you running?"

"He is not allowing anybody now!" I said, while he passed by me.

"Can't you wake up on time?" I asked, to instigate him. He had already stopped running when he heard me, but was amazed at my question. It took him a moment to respond. "Shit man! I won't be able to understand today's topic. And, I have done the assignments also."

"All this happened because of my roommate. I don't know what he was doing in the bathroom for 40 minutes!"

I have noticed that there is a category under which these beings fall. They came into existence only to study and are called study maniacs. Deprived of the practical world and real entertainment, they were always immersed in their studies. They play with equations, watch programs and eat theorems. I wonder if they shit numbers and words.

"But, why are you roaming outside?" he asked, when he realized that I was also not in class.

"Arey! I didn't do the assignment. That's why he threw me out."

Without paying any attention to my reply, he hurried to the class. I didn't know if he wanted to try for the entrance, but I was pretty sure of one thing: he wasn't going to miss any class in the year to come. I came out of the academic block to spend my next 50 minutes. I roamed about in the campus to explore areas where I hadn't been before. It was a sunny day. The bright sunrays fell straight, but because of the altitude the days were not very hot. It soothes you. With the breeze blowing, it makes the day more favorable and romantic. Sadly, I didn't have a girlfriend to enjoy all this with. After some quality time with myself, I returned for the next class. While entering, I saw some faces smiling at me sarcastically. Ignoring them, I reached out to my bench mates.

"Good Morning Mr. Pondi!" Sanjeet teased me, referencing my activity last night.

"Haha! What a joke." I said with irritation. Bhaskar and Mrinal were giggling at me. "Saale! Couldn't you wake me up in the morning?" I asked.

"You didn't ask me, man!" he replied emphatically.

"Okay. Please wake me up from tomorrow onwards. Otherwise, I will have an attendance shortage at the end!" I pleaded with him.

"Okay, buddy!" he replied simply.

Sanjeet was busy typing a text message on his phone. Getting ready for the next class, I asked him, "Hey! Whose class is this?"

"Prerna Rai!" he replied, without looking at me.

"Hey! Is it Miss Prerna's class? Schedule-wise she was to take the third period!" Nishant, who was sitting next to us, turned around in excitement and asked.

"So, what's the big deal?" I asked. Without answering me, he turned towards his bench-mates and I noticed a wave of excitement flaring up among them.

The boys became more sincere and studious in her class. It was not because she was a good teacher or took care of every student equally. It was probably because they were attracted to her. She was a striking beauty. They wanted to create a good impression on her. She was attractive. Her pleasant countenance, fair complexion and style of wearing a sari were enough to beat any good looking girl in college. Unlike most other women, she was never covered with artificial layers of make-up. She had a good figure, and was around thirty. She was, in every sense of the term, a complete Indian beauty. She entered class with a half-smile on her face. She wore a sky blue sari with silver embroidery on it. A small bindi adorned her forehead, matching the sari. Her long hair was tied in the Indian traditional style.

"Wow! Vivacious!" somebody said.

She really had a good sense of dressing and carried herself well. I was impressed by her appearance that day. Bhaskar, who sat next to me, pretended to stab himself with a make-believe knife on his heart. "Somebody, please save me today!" Sanjeet and I looked at each other. Immediately, we held Bhaskar's neck to have fun.

"We will help you die, man! Our college will be spared of one roadside Romeo!" Sanjeet said, promptly.

We left him soon, and came back to our positions as the attendance ritual began. Bhaskar was still fascinated by the ageless beauty.

Our classroom had 72 varieties of students, including 24 girls. The quality and quantity of girls in our class was good enough to have some good discussion among us boys. The first few rows were for the meritorious students and a large number of muggers. There was always a rush among the crowd as they competed to occupy the front rows. Girls didn't have a fixed seating plan in class. They sat anywhere they liked.

Our bench was for us four friends – Bhaskar, Mrinal, Sanjeet and I. We preferred to sit in any of the last rows as we found ourselves comfortable there. It was easy to have fun and indulge in gossip. It covered a variety of topics like movies, electronic gadgets, ragging, girls and many other things, but definitely not studies. It was helpful in arranging for proxy attendance for our lazy friends, depending on the strictness of the professor. Most importantly, we showed off our skills in passing spontaneous comments based on the situations.

For all these good reasons, we were 'The Backbenchers'.

Chapter Two
The hostel life

After having spent 20 days in college, which was surrounded by hills, greenery and artistic natural beauty, we were acquainted with the college and its trends, our classmates, the girls and some of the seniors who ragged us. Our friendship and bonding was intensifying in our group. We spent most of the time having fun, playing pranks and indulging in gossip in the hostel and in the classroom. The joys of a new college, studies and friends were filling us with zest. I stepped out of the academic block after completing today's lab. I was waiting for Sanjeet to come out. He was supposed to introduce me to Sabu sir, a final year senior. Sabu sir was known more famously in college by his nickname. None of us knew his real name. I heard from Sanjeet, that Sabu sir was the best and senior-most sportsperson and had been sent to present our college in the inter-college sports competition at IIT Kanpur.

"Hey Sam! What are you doing here?" Sanjeet asked me as he walked up to me.

"Nothing. Just enjoying the view. What irresistible beauty nature has!" I said.

"Good, let's go! We have to go to meet Sabu sir now," Sanjeet reminded me.

"Yeah, I know!" He led the way and I started trailing him. He seemed to be walking fast in the excitement to meet him.

"Why are you in such a hurry? Sabu sir se shaadi karne ja raha hai kya?" I asked. He slowed down.

"You know, he has won a gold medal in the race and was a runner-up in wrestling in the inter-college tournament in IIT! He came back yesterday," he couldn't stop himself from gushing about Sabu sir's achievement. "He is great!" he was as proud as he would have been had he won those medals.

"Looks like you are very inspired by him!" I asked.

"Yup. He is an all-rounder. He has a good physique, he is good at studies, and has had two placements. Most importantly, he is good at heart," Sanjeet described him well and that created a positive image in my mind, too.

"But how do you know him?" I asked.

"Arey! He is my neighbour. His father and my father are close friends," he replied pointedly, as though I should have already known that. We finally reached the hostel room. "You will see how he is, yourself!" he said to me and knocked at the door. A very lean man in a singlet with a cigarette in his fingers opened the door and peeped out. Suddenly, all my positive ideas of him vanished, when I saw him.

"Sir! Is Sabu sir inside?" Sanjeet asked; I realized that the senior who had opened the door was not Sabu sir.

The man opened the door completely and we stepped inside. I was amazed to see that there were eight seniors sitting inside, occupying all places on the bed and on a few chairs. Four of them had cigarettes in hand. The room was filled with smoke. I was frightened to see so many seniors and was sure that they were going to rag us. It wasn't going to be easy to come out safe. In the room, there were the posters of bodybuilders on the walls. There were some prizes on the shelf. Two dumb bells were placed underneath the bed. It looked like the room of a sportsperson.

"Hey Sanjeet!" A guy with a heavy build, sitting in the middle on the bed, said. I was relieved. We would have been in trouble if nobody had recognized Sanjeet. Finally, I saw what Sanjeet's meant and realized why he was called Sabu.

"Congratulations, Sabu Bhaiya!" Sanjeet congratulated him.

"Thank you!" he replied with a smile.

"Congratulations Sir!" I said, indicating that I was with Sanjeet. He nodded to thank me.

"He is my friend, Samar!" Sanjeet introduced him me and I smiled out of courtesy.

"Sit down and relax! We won't rag you!" he gestured to us to sit on the table as there was no space vacant elsewhere.

"We are completely done with ragging. Now we are in the final year!" I was relaxed. "We will be leaving in a year. The college is all yours now" he said with a sense of seniority. "Only a year is left, technically four months. We will be out of college for major projects.'

"So, technically, just a few months left!" one of them said, with some sentiment.

"I am definitely going to miss college. This college has given me a lot. I found my closest friends, a loving girl-friend and a good job, I got everything I wanted!" A handsome man spoke up. Filled with emotion, they were involved in their gossip for some time.

"So, Sanjeet! Tell me. How is everything? How about the college campus?" Sabu sir asked as he realized we were ignored while they were chattering.

"Everything is fine, Bhaiya. I love the campus. I have made some good friends here," Sanjeet said.

"Good! What about you?" he asked.

"Yeah. For me, too, everything is good here!" I was formal.

"Why are you so formal?"

"It seems you guys are being ragged by your seniors," he asked. I couldn't stop myself from replying, "Yes, sir. Almost every 3 to 4 days."

"It's very difficult to roam freely in the campus."

"Hmm… Is it severe or physical?" he asked. Physical ragging was not the usual trend in college.

"No. But they ask us to do some nonsense!" Sanjeet said.

"If you want, I can ask them to stop ragging you guys. It will be your loss!" Sabu sir responded. "Ragging gives you an opportunity to be connected with your seniors. At the end of the ragging period, they will throw a party for you. They will give you books and notes. They will advise on professors, exams and other things in college," another senior explained with utmost sincerity. "They will give you a lot of help."

"You know, my senior helped me getting a placement!" one prompted gratitude towards his senior.

"Oh! That's great!"

"By the way, we have no complaints. Everything is good for us!" Sanjeet said.

"But, still, if you find it tough to take or, if it goes physical, you can come to me," Sabu sir assured us.

"Thank you, bhaiya!" Sanjeet thanked him for the assurance.

Noticing our apprehension and pessimism, a senior stood up and came to me. He put his arm around my shoulders and started explaining it to me. "See, my friend! In the future, you will not get free time like this. After college, you will be working in some multinational company and they will suck your life out of you. You will be left with loads of work, tensions and responsibilities. At that time, you will miss your freedom, friends and fun badly. So enjoy your four years here. Make friends and have fun with them, go for outings, enjoy your hostel life! There is nothing better than that!" He said and took out a cigarette and lit it up in a unique style. I was impressed by his mannerisms.

"You will remember these four years your entire life. Make it more colourful!" It was inspiring. It made me feel proud at being a part of this college. After drawing a puff, he asked me with interest, "Do you have a girlfriend?"

"No Sir." I replied with coyness.

"Then, go for it. What are you waiting for?"

"Guru Gyani baba! How much gyan are you going to provide them today? You have to go to the academic block also!" one of the seniors with a rowdy look said.

"Okay guys. That's all from my side. I just shared my experience with you. Enjoy!" he finished.

"Okay, Sanjeet. Stay here if you want. Abhishek and I have to go to the academic block to attend a meeting with the HOD," Sabu sir said and got off the bed to leave.

"No, Bhaiya. We will also leave. We just came to congratulate you!" Sanjeet said with a smile.

"Thank you, sir! It was a nice experience!" I said.

"Wah! Guru has made one shishya. Jai ho Abhishek baba ki!" a senior snickered. Now, I learned his name.

"Hey! Come anytime you feel like!" Sabu sir said as we stepped out of his room.

"Sure, Bhaiya!" Sanjeet said and we came out.

"Wow! It was a great experience!" I whispered.

"I told you, right?" he looked proud.

"I was impressed by Abhishek sir. I liked his speech, his style of smoking. I have seen that many seniors are smoking! Is that also a trend here?"

Sanjeet looked at me.

"You know, I get fascinated when I see people smoking in style," I said. "Once, I tried smoking with one of my school friends. But, that was just to experience the taste!"

He smiled at my fascination for smoking. "Saale, you are very filmi!" he said.

"Hey! Let's have it tonight. Let's go out and bring a packet of cigarette. Mrinal and Bhaskar will also like it!" I suggested impulsively.

"No. I haven't smoked before!" he was hesitant.

"Don't worry. Bhaskar will help us. He occasionally smokes. Nothing will happen."

"But, it is injurious to health!" he was still hesitating.

"Oh! Come on! Don't talk like a kid. We will have it occasionally!" I insisted. It worked.

"Okay. Let's go!" he agreed. We started walking towards the Pan-shop, outside the campus.

Discussing those seniors and cigarette brands we reached the shop, bought a large packet of cigarettes and came back to the hostel. It didn't take much time. I told Bhaskar and Mrinal about the plan and they took it with interest. We decided to have it after dinner. We didn't want any senior to rag us, as the chances of their coming were high because it was the weekend. To be on the safe side, we waited till 11:00 PM. Thankfully, no senior entered our territory. I couldn't control myself any longer and took out the cigarettes.

"Hey! Let's wait for half-an-hour more! We should start at 11:30 PM," Bhaskar was skeptical.

"Don't worry, boy! Nobody will come now."

"We will see if anybody comes!" Sanjeet was confident. I already knew where he got that confidence from.

With a rising sense of thrill, Bhaskar and I lit up the cigarettes. Mrinal and Sanjeet decided to share it with us. Bhaskar took the first puff lightly and exhaled looking outside the window.

"Hmm… It's good!" he said. With the second one, he showed us how to smoke.

Mine was half-lit. To light it up properly I drew a heavy puff, which caused slight giddiness. My blood circulation hiked up. I had never experienced such feeling before. Bhaskar passed it to Sanjeet and he smoked like Bhaskar did, but he choked hard.

"Go slow!" Bhaskar instructed. I passed it to Mrinal and he smoked well. That night, the entire group experienced the flavour of smoking. After that round, we opened the gates and windows to let the smell out of room.

"So, how did you feel?" Bhaskar asked Sanjeet. He did not reply as he was still experiencing the aftereffect.

"Tujhe cigarette chad gayi hai kya?" I joked and everybody laughed.

"As if you have been smoking since childhood!" he retorted. "But yaar! It feels like dizziness when you have it!"

"Yes. I also felt the same," Mrinal agreed.

"Don't worry. Nothing will happen. That happens only at the beginning," Bhaskar assured us.

"Then after some time we will have another round!" I said with a silly excitement. Nobody responded. "Hey! After the ragging period is over, we can smoke freely in our rooms, right?" I asked.

"Yes! After that, you can do anything you feel!" Bhaskar said assertively.

"We will do all the things we aren't able to do now. We can have a grand party in our hostel rooms. It will be full of drinking, smoking, hooting and shouting!" Sanjeet was ready with his wish.

"I will work hard to get a girlfriend. It's my dream to have a girlfriend in college. I will make some friends among the girls at least," I said.

"As if they are all waiting for you!" Sanjeet said.

"Seriously! A lot of beautiful girls are there in our college." Mrinal said. "I like Aditi and Rashmi. I will try to be friends with them, initially." And then, the conversation continued.

"Rashmi is better. But the only problem is that she is a local."

"So what?"

"Itna chalta hai, yaar!"

"I like Amrita Jain, she is beautiful and cute."

"Oh! Section D, right?"

"Yes."

"Yes, she is beautiful."

"What about Tripti Dandekar?"

"Oho! Yes! Yes!"

"She is a real hottie."

"She looks so sexy!"

"Haan yaar."

"But you know, figure-wise, no one can beat Sakshi Singh."

"Oh my god, her curves are awesome."

"Really…"

"And, she looks best in western outfits."

"Whatever you say, my Arpita is the best."

"My Arpita?"

"I mean, I like her yaar."

"Hmm..."

"And, who is that girl?"

"The girl who wears cargo pants, and always has chewing gum in her mouth?"

"Which girl?"

"Yesterday I showed you one, right?"

"Okay. I got it."

"She is a third year senior."

"Oh! Senior!"

"But, personally I feel like Shilpi Bansal is best in the town."

"Who Shilpi?"

"That second year senior whose picture in on the magazine cover this year."

"Okay. So, she is Shilpi Bansal!"

"I had a chance to talk to her. A group of seniors were ragging me, and she was there in the group."

"She is beautiful, sexy and cute, all in one piece."

"Is it? I haven't seen her before. Show me her tomorrow."

"Okay."

"But for me, Prerna Rai is the best."

"Hmm... No one can beat her in Indian traditional dressing style."

"But, saale, she is our teacher."

That night, we had another round of smokes and gossiped about girls. It was more interesting than any ordinary night we spent before. We became chain smokers from that night on. Excited with the discussion on girls, Mrinal decided to talk to Rashmi the very next day.

The next day, we went on an evening walk on Maal Road for Mrinal's plan to take shape.

"What are you going to do? Will you directly talk to her or do you have a plan?" I asked.

"Yes bro! I will take a written introduction from her with a trick, saying that seniors have asked me to do it so as a part of the ragging," he said confidently.

"Really! What if you get caught? What if she asks the name of the senior?" I asked.

"Nothing will happen. If she asks, I will make up a name. She is not going to confirm, right?" he was confident. "You can also come with me," he asked me to join.

"No. I am fine."

"At least come with me for moral support. You can stay at some distance," he insisted.

"Okay. That I can do!" We started searching for her on Maal Road. Mrinal was sure he would find her somewhere there, since on a daily basis, she took a walk with her friends on Maal road.

After a complete round of Maal Road, we found her sitting at the stairs of front exit of the Academic block, with one of her friends.

Mrinal went up to execute his plan. I stayed some distance away, from where I could watch all of it.

"All the best!" I wished him.

Mrinal reached her with a sorry face and started describing the false story with an artificial expression to Rashmi and her friend. I was amazed to see that his trick worked as they were talking casually and wrote their introduction for him. Before he came back, he thanked them and they shared a mutual smile. I was flabbergasted with his smartness and trick.

Apart from the trick, another obvious reason for his confidence and success was his handsome appearance. His personality could easily attract and convince anyone.

"Great yaar! How do you get this much confidence?" I asked him, impressed. He shrugged with a smile.

Despite the acknowledgment of its positive results, I wasn't able to find the guts to do the same thing myself.

Chapter Three

A new girl in the city

It was the first class of the day when Sanjeet and I entered the Basic Electronics Lab. It was the only lab that aroused some interest in me. I always had an affinity for wires and circuits, which made me enjoy doing the experiments. It is a fact that labs are always interesting and livelier than lectures are. As we entered, we saw a new girl sitting beside the lab instructor and talking to him. She was showing something like a letter, or perhaps a document, to him.

"Hmm! Who is this girl yaar?" I mumbled.

"I think she is from a different section and might have come to clarify her doubts. You know how girls are concerned about their studies," Sanjeet replied. "Let's start with our experiments. Please complete it early today, so that we can go for a sutta- break. I know you will do it diligently!" he said with a shrewd smile.

We had an understanding that we would individually try to learn the subjects that we were good at earnestly, and then we could exchange notes later on. The trick worked. He always assisted me with the subjects like Engineering Drawing, which I was not good at. I helped him with theories and labs of circuits and wires. It helped make things uncomplicated and easier. After a conversation that lasted five minutes, the lab instructor seemed satisfied with the documents that the girl had showed him. By then, we had occupied our seats and were about to begin our experiments. I turned around to find the lab instructor ready to address us. "Attention everyone! We have a new student. Meet your new classmate, Sanjana Dixit!" He pointed at her, as if he had known her for a long time. She smiled broadly at all of us. "She has joined the batch late and was absent for the past few classes and lab sessions. She will be regular from today onwards. Please help her with the already covered experiments and topics in labs and classes!"

Sanjeet and I shared a glance with cunning smiles on our faces. The idea behind the smile was that since our roll numbers were allotted according to the alphabetical order of our names, it would mean that Sanjana's name would fall between mine and Sanjeet's. Earlier Sanjeet had told me from his database updates that a girl named Sanjana had the roll number after mine.

"Roll Number 41, Samar Singh and 43, Sanjeet Kumar. Please come here!" the lab instructor called us. We left out places in a jiffy and went up to him. "Sanjeet! Sanjana's roll number is 42 and yours is 43. So, she will group with Samar. You will pair up with Sujoy Ghosh in this lab," he said.

Sanjeet was shocked at the announcement. We didn't foresee this. There was nothing he could say. "Okay sir!" he agreed. Sanjeet could not argue with the instructor as he was caught not doing his experiment in the previous class, and was not able to answer the basic questions that the lab instructor had asked him.

"It will be useful for you. He will explain all the fundamentals and make your work easier," he said, trying to manipulate the situation. Sanjeet left, disappointed, to shift his place. I was also upset for a bit, but there was some eagerness at the prospect of connecting with the new girl, too.

"Samar!" the lab instructor said. I looked at him attentively. "As I mentioned, she is new in this batch. Please help her with the experiments completed so far. Give her the notes for the previous classes as well."

"Sure sir."

"You will have to work hard to cover the topics that have been done so far," he told Sanjana.

"Yes sir."

"You may start today's lab experiment." he said.

"Thank you, sir!" We turned around to go back to our places.

"Hi! I am Samar!" I said, smiling.

"Hi!" she said, half-smiling as she looked at me for a second. It seemed like she was less considerate about my introduction. A kind of unease and nervousness flared up on her face. It may have been because it was a new place. I looked at her from the corner of my eye. She had a pretty face and a wheatish complexion. We reached our place. My notebook was on the desk and the infamous "F" word was written on it in block letters. I hurriedly kept it inside my bag, cleared the desk and offered her a seat.

"Thank you!" Her smile was broader and more natural this time. Girls usually take their time to adjust to a new environment or a new friendship. They always come to anything with loads of emotions and tons of baggage. One has to adjust with all that. I am not sure if it is a merit or demerit, but it creates spice in a relationship.

I brought the equipment from the lab technician for the experiment. She was preparing herself for the lab. She untied her bun, allowing her hair to cascade onto her shoulders. She wiped her face with a handkerchief, glanced around the lab and then let out a sigh of relief. Finally, she was ready to accept her new environment.

"So, how do you find the new place?" I asked. It was perhaps too early to ask. But I thought it would make her feel comfortable.

"So far, it has been good. I haven't roamed around the campus yet. I came here this morning with my father."

"Okay. I am sure you will love it. The campus and college environment are fabulous. The evening charm of Maal Road is something else! It is awesome here," I said. She smiled at my description.

I was excited that she had joined. I started setting up the equipment. While I was at it, somebody patted my shoulder and whispered in my right ear, "Beta! Ladki dikhi nahin ki dost ko bhul gaye. Koi nahin, aj raat mein class lagegi teri!" I turned around to see Sanjeet. I stood up and dragged him back to his desk whispering, "Abey, she is a newcomer. She doesn't know anything!"

"Hmm… I see!" he replied, looking at me with sarcasm. "That's okay. I was just joking, man. Start the experiment. Do explain it to me later. It is very difficult to do it with this idiot!" he said with a hint of despair, pointing at his new partner. "He has hijacked the equipment and is trying to do all the nonsense he thinks he knows. When I asked, he tried to explain it and I couldn't understand a word! Bullshit!" Sanjeet was miffed.

"Okay. Okay. Chill! I will explain everything to you after I am done with mine. Okay?"

"Thanks, yaar! Now go. Enjoy your time with her!" he said, with a smile. "And listen!" I doubled back. He whispered, "I know that you are the typical "Lallu" type and she is beautiful. You still have a good chance because you are good here at the lab. You can impress her with that. You lucky bastard!" he said, patting me on my back. I smiled with pride.

"Nothing like that!" I said and returned to my place. I noticed that my lab partner was looking at the Zener Diode with interest, holding it in her hand.

"This is the Zener Diode. We need it for today's experiment," I said. "Our experiment is to study the forward and reverse bias voltage-ampere characteristics of the Zener Diode, and to determine the breakdown voltage, static voltage and dynamic resistances." She stared at me, perplexed, like she was completely oblivious to what I had said. Her expression impelled me to explain some basics on the lab and the equipment we used. She listened carefully, nodding occasionally, and at times repeating some of my words, as if she was familiar with the concept. I liked all of it.

Girls are very good with their expressions. They are gifted in this art. For example, you will rarely be able to know if a girl is on her period unless she tells you explicitly. She will only tell you that she has a stomach ache or a headache. Probably that's why people say that girls are unpredictable. It takes a long time to understand them. With her sincere expressions, she watched me doing the experiment. I guessed that she was tired and wanted to leave early. Keeping that in mind, I completed the experiment fast. When I told her the last reading, a big smile erupted on her face. She looked at me, impressed, as I was the first one to complete the experiment.

"Thank you for your help," she said, genuinely.

"You are welcome!" I replied. Sincere smiles were exchanged between us. This filled me with confidence and excitement. "Don't forget to bring your lab file next time, with this experiment written in it. You can take the readings from me anytime."

"Sure Samar!" For the first time, she said my name with a sense of friendliness. I was filled with pride at my knowledge. She left, and it happened that she looked more beautiful and friendly to me when I recalled her in my thoughts. "She is good!" I whispered to myself. Sanjeet's idea that I had a chance to impress her filled me with excitement and hope. It was almost certain that she was going to be my lab partner at least for this semester. The change of events and new friends filled me with delight. I hoped to see a new Samar. After lunch, I joined my group at the backbench for the next class.

"Hey! I won the bet. MAN U lost the match yesterday!" Bhaskar rejoiced, telling Mrinal about the football match. "What a goal! What a goal by Ronaldo!"

"Okay. I will buy you a packet of cigarettes this evening. Let's see what happens in the next match!" Mrinal replied with a hint of revenge.

Bhaskar and Mrinal were hardcore football fans, especially for the county matches. Chelsea, MAN U, Real Madrid, Messi, Ronaldo, Rooney – we were familiar with these terms as they were always involved in heated discussions after any of these matches. They always made their bets for a packet of cigarettes during the match. Other students watched cricket, but these two loved football. Mrinal used to say, "Football is best game in the world. It is poetry in motion!" They participated in football tournaments held in and outside the college. This was why Bhaskar and Mrinal were closer to each other. Suddenly, the noise came down to some extent when the Physics teacher walked in with a bundle of notes and four chalk pieces in hand.

Suddenly it struck me. Where was Sanjana? She should have joined for the post lunch session, but I couldn't find her. I started looking around impatiently. Just then, she appeared at the entrance, seeking permission to get in. "May I come in Sir?" she asked softly. All eyes turned to her and a round of murmuring started. She entered after he gave her permission and sat down on the second last bench of the right column. Everybody, including my bench mates, were still staring at her.

"Seven out of ten. I give her seven," Bhaskar announced his score after looking at her. "What do you say guys?"

"Yes, she is good. But, who is she? Is she a newcomer?" Mrinal asked curiously.

"Yes," Sanjeet said. "Doston! Be respectful about her. She is our Sam's new lab partner."

"Achha!" Mrinal and Bhaskar exclaimed looking at me. They didn't know the story as they were in different lab sections.

"How and when did it happen?" Bhaskar asked.

Without waiting for my reply, Sanjeet told them everything in his style. I chose to keep quiet as they were in the mood to tease me, especially Sanjeet. The roll call started but everybody was busy gossiping with their bench-mates. Our Physics teacher was lenient. Being a newcomer, Sanjana was asked to introduce herself after the roll call. The class turned silent as she spoke up. "Good Afternoon Sir, and good afternoon friends! My name is Sanjana Dixit. I am from Ranchi, Jharkhand. I completed my higher secondary from S.K.V. School in Jamshedpur. I have joined this college in the Electronics and Communications stream."

"Good! But why did you join so late?" the teacher asked.

"Sir, I didn't get my branch of choice in the first round of counseling here. I was trying my luck at other colleges. After 20 days, I was given a seat here for this branch as a student had left college and I was first in the waiting list!"

"Good. Sit down," said the teacher, least interested in her story, anyway. "See, so far, we have covered until Surface Tension. Catch up on the topics covered so far because I will be conducting a test next week."

"What!" I screamed all of a sudden. The entire class was equally shocked to know that it was going to be our first test this semester. I was completely blank on the subject. Sanjeet and I looked at each other in anxiety.

"You can come to me anytime for your doubts," the teacher was busy telling Sanjana.

She was completely perplexed, too. This was her first class and she was greeted with the possibility of a test. I could see the tension and anxiety building up on her cute face. She started biting her nails and looking around. Finally, her eyes found me staring at her. Recalling the morning, she smiled at me, and waved slightly. I responded with a smile. I liked the way the day had started. It was new and inspiring. Her innocent eyes and nervous smile drew my attention.

Chapter Four
The laughter

The bell rang by end of the third period. After a long and hectic schedule, I was not in the right mood to attend the fourth one. I told Mrinal that we could bunk the next class and smoke a cigarette and drink tea. But Sanjeet refused. "No Sam. We have just one period left. I don't want to find myself with an attendance problem at the end! By the way its Dubey sir's class, which means fun."

"Come on! Sit and enjoy!" Mrinal said.

Mr. Chakradhar Dubey taught Engineering Math classes for first year students. He was a short man and terribly old fashioned. He was an expert in his subject, though. His most interesting feature was his weak grammar and native accent in his English, which always gave us plenty of things to make fun of.

"Oh No! Not this time. I can't tolerate that *maid* guy!" I said, exasperated. We used to call him "maid" as he always pronounced mad as *maid*.

"I need a break. Let me go out. Please give my attendance by proxy!" I stood up to leave. I had noticed that other students always enjoyed his class but, I found it irritating. Sanjeet and Mrinal sat beside me. They intentionally crossed me sideways and did not allow me to leave. "We won't let you go Mr. Sam. You have to enjoy the madness with us!" Sanjeet said as he started pulling my shirt.

I responded aggressively. I tried to get out of his grasp by crossing over the desk. Continuing on their own trajectory of amusement, they started pulling me forcefully. In the meantime, the "maid" guy entered class. A sudden silence fell. Everybody stood up as is the usual ritual in greeting a teacher. I stood with one leg out of the desk and one inside, sitting on the desk. With a quick move, I tried to get inside, but those bastards started pushing me out for fun. "Let me inside, you idiots!" I whispered to them.

"What is going there?" A loud voice broke the silence. Dubey sir was addressing me. I looked up at him with an innocent expression. Everybody stood in position. I sat on the desk with my one leg inside and one outside. "You! What is your name? What are you trying to do?" I decided to answer the first one as I didn't have an answer for the second.

"Sir, Samar," I said.

"Is this answer of my *qostion*?" he asked. "I know this is summer. But, what are you trying to do?" I was perplexed, while everyone else was desperately trying to hide his laughter. In the meantime, he gestured to the others to sit down. I took advantage of the situation and got inside. I murmured angrily to Sanjeet and Mrinal, "I will take care of the both of you after class." Ignoring what I said, they were making fun of me.

Dubey Sir started screaming at me. "You know manners? Or you have come from *bhillage* (village)?"

I chose to keep quiet. The others were busy snickering.

"Everyone!" he screamed, addressing the class while I stood rooted to the spot. "Any boy or girl make noise in class, will be viewed seriously!" He clearly had no idea what he was saying. "And you! Not do this from next time! Now *Shit* down." Everyone started laughing, looking at me as if I had done something funny. I sat down and realized that the session was indeed one that was not to be missed out on.

"Aye! Kya karta hai tum log?" he was aggressive now. "Do not make noise. Just now I saw, the principal has *Passed Away* in the corridor!" Everyone burst out laughing, me included. But he couldn't understand why.

"Quiet!" he yelled. "Why do you laugh? Anybody laugh or talk, I will throw out!" The class suddenly became silent. Dubey sir then took out his book with an annoyed look on his face. He was about to teach us the next theorem. At the same time, Manoj appeared at the entrance to the classroom, asking to be allowed to enter.

"See, these students! Come late in class!" He was fuming. "How you will pass *igzaam* (exam)? How you will make your *carrier* (career)? You idiots! Why you came late?"

"Sir, today was the last day to pay my fees. There was a long queue for it," Manoj said with a sorry face.

"Okay. Come in," he said, satisfied with the reply he had gotten. Dubey sir turned towards the blackboard to write. He started explaining and proving theorems with his usual droning voice. We imitated him behind his back and chuckled to our heart's content. During the session, occasionally, I stole a few glances at Sanjana. She was laughing, too. She had looked at me a couple of times with a pitiful expression while Dubey sir yelled at me. Her childlike giggles and alluring charms were attractive. She was dressed in black, and wore matching earrings. The stark black was a striking contrast with her fair beauty. Her beautifully arched eyebrows and deep eyes made me tingle. I noticed that while writing, she tilted her head slightly, which made her hair fall freely. She would tuck a stray strand behind her ear every now and then. I couldn't help but feel a sense of affection for her.

Struggling with the chalk and board, Dubey sir was busy proving a complicated theorem. A hint of confidence flared up on his face as soon as he completed it, which got him to play a question-answer round with us.

Only some students were able to answer him correctly, as nobody had paid attention in his classes. He was miffed at those who couldn't answer. He asked them to stand up and started giving them his hilarious life lessons.

"Why you students don't study? See *gaaiz* (guys)! You are not doing correct. Making good *carrier* (career) is not a child play. You need to work hard for that. Wasting time with *girl-phriend* (girlfriends), watching *flims* (films), gossiping and playing games at *haastel* (hostel)! All these will destroy your *carrier* (career). Don't divert! Your *phocus* (focus) should always be on studies. Never shy your parents. Always feel them proud!" He pumped his fist in the air for emphasis.

The combination of his expressions, his accent and the meaning of his speech made us all laugh.

"It is my duty to see you correct path. And I work hard for that. Remember one thing! This is not a *phun* (fun) class. Try to *under-us-tand* (understand) what I teach, *becaause* (because) this will only help you in the *igzaam* (exam). If you find *daut* (doubt), come to me anytime. I will solve. But study hard. Ok?" he looked around, trying to see if we agreed.

"Okay, sir!" Some of the sincere students replied in low voices. After a completely fun session, we stepped out of class, gossiping about his hilarious speech. Everybody discussed the session, and was chortling. All of us went for lunch. It was a relief that we didn't have any class in the next half of the day. We returned to our hostel rooms after lunch. As soon as I changed my clothes and got into a relaxing mood, specifically to watch a movie on Mrinal's laptop, Bhaskar popped in to the room and said, "Hey Sam! I have to pay my fees yaar. Today is the last day. Come with me, na?"

"No! Please... Not me." I said with a miserable expression on my face. As soon as Bhaskar said that, Mrinal took out his phone and went out of the room, pretending to attend a call and Sanjeet acted like his stomach was upset, and that he needed to go to attend the nature's call.

"Han Saalon! I will take care of all of you!" Bhaskar said, noticing everyone. Nobody wanted to spoil their free time and to waste an hour uselessly standing in the queue with him. Hopelessly, he came to me. "You are my only friend here. Come with me, na? Please!" Bhaskar put his hand around my shoulder.

"This is injustice! Fine. Okay. I will come!" I said bleakly. In some time, we left for the fees counter in the academic block. There was just five minutes left for the afternoon sessions to start. Some students were already standing in queue. Bhaskar trailed them. I stood beside him for his amusement as that was what I was called there for. It is a sweet fact that there are many surprising advantages and support you receive in friendship. In return, you have to bear some obligations, too. But that's what friendship is all about. Overall, we were savouring the friendship in our group.

After waiting for 10 minutes in the queue, we saw the fee collector at the counter. The queue had stretched by around 20 meters longer. As soon as the queue started moving, Sanjana had joined it. A smile found its way on my face. Bhaskar couldn't understand it. When I told him why, he said, "Okay! See, I am your true friend! I knew she was going to come here, that's why I had you come along!" he joked, taking advantage of the situation. "Are you hitting on her?"

"Nothing like that, yaar!" I said.

"Anyway, she is good looking. And you have a good chance too as you are her lab partner."

"Hmm."

She hadn't noticed my presence there and was looking at the long queue with frustration on her face. Her impatience enhanced her cuteness.

"Bhaskar, she is getting frustrated waiting there, standing at the end of the queue," I said.

"So? Go ahead and entertain her!" Bhaskar replied sarcastically.

"No yaar. I am going to offer her a favour. She can come behind or ahead of you in the line, so she will not have to stand for long in the queue!"

"Acha! To aag yahan tak lag gayi hai?" Bhaskar joked.

"Okay. I'm going now, I'll be back in two minutes." I walked towards Sanjana. She noticed me and smiled.

"Hi!" I said when I reached her. She greeted me with a big smile.

"How are you?" I asked.

"Okay," she said without much enthusiasm.

"So, what are you doing here? I mean... Are you here to pay your fees?"

It made her giggle. "Obviously!" she said. The guys standing behind her were looking at us, probably thinking I was hitting on her.

"You can join us there. My friend is standing in the queue!" I offered, pointing at Bhaskar.

"Umm..." she tilted her face and assessed the queue. For formality's sake, she refused. "No. Thanks! I will manage."

"Arey it's okay! He is Bhaskar, our classmate. No issues. Come!"

"Okay. Where is he?" She asked, coming out of the queue. Without replying, I took her to Bhaskar. He was just one place behind the counter and was busy counting the amount he had to pay as fees. "Hey Bhasu! This is Sanjana, our classmate."

"Oh... Hi!"

"Hi!" Sanjana greeted him with a smile.

"She was standing at the end of the queue, so I brought her here," I said.

"Yeah, sure! I am just one place behind." Bhaskar took a step back and she entered the queue before him. Because everyone was a fresher in the queue, nobody opposed this.

"Thank you Bhaskar!" she said with a smile.

"You are welcome!" Bhaskar replied with a gentlemen's smile.

Within a couple of minutes, she reached the counter and paid her fees. She came out of the queue and Bhaskar went up next. I joined her and received a genuine word of thanks from her.

"So... How is everything going?" I asked as we walked slowly.

"Everything is new but I am settling down slowly. The only thing bothering me is that I have joined late and many topics have already been taught. There is going to be a test next week!" she seemed worried. "I don't know what I will do. I haven't gotten the notes, either!" she sighed in disappointment.

"Hey! Don't worry. I will help you." I said. "You can take my notes. If you find any difficulty in understanding any of it, I can help you." I realized that I spoke as if I was one of the toppers of the college. "I mean... I will study and then explain it to you."

"Okay. That's cool!" she agreed. "For now, if I can get the notes for Physics, that would be a great help as we have a test next week!"

"Anytime, Sanjana! Take my number and call me when you need anything." I gave her my number. I did not ask for her cell number thinking that I would get her number once she called me.

"Okay, can you bring it to me this evening?" she asked.

"Sure. Give me a call ten minutes before you need it."

"Okay. Thanks Samar! I will call you!" I was happy that she was ready to accept my assistance. That could open up more opportunities for me to impress her. "Bye!" she said.

I turned around and found that Bhaskar was standing at some distance, leaning against the pillar and waiting for our conversation to end. As soon as I indicated him, he joined me and we left for our rooms.

In the evening I got a call from her while I was relaxing in my room. After a short conversation with her on the call, I stood up, borrowed Bhaskar's Physics notebook and headed towards the A-block, where she had asked me to come. I was glad that I had her number – it was important to start a good friendship with her. When I reached A-block, I found her standing with another girl, with whom I wasn't acquainted. It was disappointing, for if Sanjana was alone there, I could have initiated some personal and informal conversation with her.

"Hi Samar!" she said as soon as I reached them. "She is Komal, my roommate," she introduced the girl next to her.

"Hello!" I greeted.

"Actually we are coming from the dispensary; she is not feeling well," Sanjana said.

"Oh! What happened?" I asked.

"Nothing serious. She had a stomach ache. The doctor has given her medicines," she said. I guessed in my mind what the exact problem she might have had.

"Okay. Do get some rest!" I said to Komal. After that, there was a sudden silence. I could not understand how to start a conversation, so I gave her the notebook and said, "The notes on almost all the topics are written here. If you have any questions, call me."

"Okay, thanks!" She didn't try to hold on to the conversation, perhaps because of Komal's presence.

"Okay. Bye!" I said and left in disappointment.

I reached my room. After sometime, following our daily engagement, I went outside the campus with my group. We ordered some snacks, tea and our regular brand of cigarettes and started chatting and playing pranks on each other at the Ohm's shop. Today I was targeted by them and Bhaskar was the initiator. I wasn't annoyed by their pranks. I was happy at being linked with Sanjana.

Within a couple of minutes, my phone vibrated, signaling a text message. It was from Sanjana. A smile spread on my face as I read it.

"Thanks 4 d notes! ☺ Is it fine if I return it tomorrow evening?"

This was completely unexpected. I thought she would not start any conversation first. It filled me with ebullience. I replied saying:

"Sure. Anytime. So, started studyin?"

I received a message while walking on the way back to our rooms:

"No samar! Going to. Wat about u?"

We started exchanging texts at regular intervals. Sometimes, texting works better than verbal conversations. It saves you from facial expressions that may give you away, and gives you the time to think and present yourself in fun ways.

I replied saying:

"Nope. I hav to. N anyway we have time for it. So, any plans for weekend?"

After an hour she said,

"Nothin specific. Tomorrow I may go out for shopping. Utensils and books. Wat about u? This subject is killing me Samar! ☹"

I liked the way conversation was progressing. I replied saying:

"Hmm... Okay. 2morrow I may also go out for movi with frens. And no plans for Sunday, may be some study work."

She said:

"Wow! Which movie?"

I wrote back quickly saying:

"Bachna ae haseeno... Ranbir Kapoor."

Some time passed before I had her next reply. Then, we continued one after another saying:

"Great... njy. I am tryin to understand the idiotic concepts of Physics. But, its too tough... ☹"

I said:

"U can try to understand the first chapter as that is very theoretical. N I can explain the secnd and thrd on Sunday, if u want..."

Sanjana: *"Really? I wud like to!"*

Me: *"Yeah. Np."*

Sanjana: *"ok. Then, Sunday mrning we wl go smwhere.*

Me: *"Sure. Then morning 11. Ok?"*

Sanjana: *"Ok. Thanks Samar! Bye… GN"*

Me: *"☺… Gud Nt."*

The texting session had ended. We were now relaxing in our rooms. Busy with my group mates in various activities, I was smiling inwardly, wondering how different and eventful my day was today from every other ordinary day.

Chapter Five

My first Date

Although I was studying till late last night, I woke up early this morning. All that hard work was done for my study with Sanjana today. It was a Sunday and I was ready by 10:30 AM. But the others, including my roommates, were still asleep. It was too early to get ready for me, too, on a Sunday. But, everything was fair for my first study session-cum-date with Sanjana. It took a whole hour to get dressed in my best outfit with all extra effort such as the selection of my clothes, washing my face, dabbing on some hair gel and spraying deodorant on myself. After all my extra-curricular activities to make an impression on her, I realized that she hadn't called me yet to confirm.

Then, finally at 10:45 AM, I called her to confirm.

"Hello! Sanjana! Good morning! Are you ready?" I asked.

"Yeah, Samar! I was about to call you. I am almost ready. Give me 10 minutes."

"Sure. Take your time."

"You can come outside the girls' hostel. We can start from there."

"Okay Sanjana. I will be there in 10 minutes."

"Okay then, bye!"

"Bye"

After that, I just looked myself in the mirror once again and left the room without telling my group as they would have started teasing me if they knew about my outing. With impulsive excitement, I speedily headed towards the girls' hostel. Sharp at 11:00 AM, I stood outside the girls' hostel. Previously, I used to see guys waiting outside the girls' hostel for their girlfriends, which always made me feel low about not having a girlfriend. Though I didn't have one now, too, it gave me a sense of pride that I was waiting for someone there. After a minute, I saw her coming out in a white top and a pair of blue jeans, carrying a brown purse, with light make up on her face. She was real hot! Her figure was more apparent and attractive in this outfit. I had never seen her in western clothes before because as per the ragging rules we were allowed to wear only formals inside the college premises.

"Hey Samar! You look so fresh."

"Thanks! I woke up early today!"

"So, where are we going now?"

"Where would you like to go?" I asked her.

"Umm..." Tapping her index finger on her cheek, she said, "We can go to CCD or, the Bake House or, we can go to Fun and food Zone. What do you say?"

Girls are always like this. They can never pick one. I loved her way of speaking; it was so childlike and cute.

"Today is Sunday. These places will be crowded. And, if they notice us there, we will get caught for ragging. Then, instead of our study time it will become their entertainment time."

"Is it?" she asked and I nodded in response. "Then, where can we go?"

"We can go to Baba Paratha, behind the campus where freshers visit. Parathas and tea are very good there. We can have our study session peacefully there."

Girls usually hesitate to go at the places with a name like "Baba Paratha". But then she agreed. "If seniors get us, it will be a complete wastage of time. Let's go to Baba Paratha!"

It was a sunny day and it was beautiful. Occasionally, when a light breeze blew, it carried her fragrance along.

I was engrossed in her charms. She asked me, "You guys have good fun sitting in the last bench… Hai naa?

"Yeah! We always have a lot of fun in class, the hostel and outside. Sanjeet, Bhaskar and Mrinal are my classmates, bench mates and group mates. We are close friends!"

"Great! You are having a good time here, I guess."

"Yup!" I smiled thinking that going on a date with a girl like her was also a good time for me.

"What about you? New friends? Any new group?" I asked.

"Umm… Nothing like that yet. I have a good bonding with CR Pallavi. Komal is a good roommate. I don't have any friends among the boys except for you." I was happy that she counted on me as a friend.

With this friendly success, I couldn't stop admiring myself. "Good going Sam!" I told myself. After walking for 15 minutes, we reached. It seemed that Sanjana had never been to a place like that before. She looked around with a keen interest. It was an open area enclosed by a bamboo shed. Pebbles were laid on the ground with some greenery. A handful of freshers hung around in the last rows. She chose to take the second table. The waiter, Raku, came to take the orders.

"You can order whatever you like. I am okay with everything!" she said.

We can only get Parathas with great taste here and I am sure you will like it." I said.

"Okay! Let's see!"

"Bhai, garamaa garam do gobhi parathe, do aloo parathe, aur do chai le aana," I said. Raku nodded and left. A minute passed without any conversation.

"So… Ma'am! Tell me something about yourself."

"Achha…" she smiled, as if she had caught my intentions.

"First, you tell me what you know about me. Then I will tell you what you don't know!" she said.

"Okay. So, you want to hear your praises!"

"Nothing like that."

"Okay. Let's begin. Sanjana Dixit. A girl from Ranchi, who has joined this college in Electronics and Communication stream."

"Okay." She was smiling.

"She likes to listen to music and watching movies." I guessed.

"That's right."

"She is sweet and beautiful."

"Hmmm. Flirting haan?"

"Her smile is so bright that it lights up the lights."

"Oh... Please! Stop your false praises." She was still smiling.

"Her best friend is Samar Singh alias Sam."

"Oho... ho! I never said that Mr. Samar Singh alias Sam!" She laughed again.

"And... She is a good girl."

"How can you say that? You hardly know me!"

"I know!" I said confidently. "That's enough of mine. Now, it's your turn."

"Tell me your story, boy!"

"There is nothing to tell you about me. I am what I am. I am how I look, what I speak, the way I behave – straight and simple. That's it."

"Also, you are good to me! You helped me since my first day in college. You made me feel comfortable here! You are a nice guy, Sam!" She said gently. I was overwhelmed.

"Thank you!" I replied. She had really made my day.

Raku came with the orders. We realized that we hadn't even started studying. I was enjoying our conversation. Raku kept our food before us and left.

"Okay! We will start our Physics session after eating the famous Baba Parathas!" I said. She nodded and we took single Parathas on our plates. After eating a morsels, she said, "Hmmm... It is really good! I love this place, yaar!"

"I told you na..." I said. She took another paratha and smiled at me.

"By the way, we are not done with your autobiography yet. You can tell me things I should know about you, being a friend!" She looked at me intently and smiled for a moment.

"There is nothing like that, Sam! You know everything!"

She took a few minutes to collect her thoughts. "I have started enjoying college life." She looked happy. "I was fed up of school. The dress code, school bag with a tiffin box, discipline! A list of instructions and suggestions from teachers and parents! Oh my god! Here I can do what I want. I love my freedom very much!"

"Okay. So, Sanjana is an independent and free girl now! I am always there to fight for your freedom. My grandfather was a freedom fighter!" She laughed out loud. I loved the way she laughed. It was so natural, so childlike.

We started study session just after eating. I explained the core concepts of Engineering Physics and gave her examples. I took one-and-a-half hours to cover the syllabus for the test, and had another round of tea with her. She paid attention sincerely. I noticed that she had understood the concepts well. After a lovely session which lasted three hours, we came back to the campus. To see her off for the day, I walked her to the girls' hostel.

"I know what you will say now. But no thank you and no sorry between us!" I said.

"Okay, but, who said I was going to thank you?" she giggled. I liked that she was getting closer to me.

"Bye Sam! I will see you tomorrow in class."

"Bye!" I said, and kept looking at her till she had gone inside.

Chapter Six

The Party night

Everybody was familiar with my friendship with Sanjana. My friends were teasing me for it. I observed that Sanjeet was a bit envious of her as our bond in the lab was broken after she joined. He had seen us sharing smiles and gossiping more than doing experiments in the lab. But, I enjoyed the unexpected and sweet change. A week after our session at Baba Paratha, we had the surprise Physics test. I managed to answer most of the questions, but I eagerly wanted to know the results of my hard work for Sanjana.

"Hey Sanjana!" I called her when she was stepping out of class with Pallavi after the test. They turned around to me.

"Hi!" I greeted them and smiled in courtesy.

"Hi Samar!" Pallavi replied.

"How was your test?" I asked.

"Yeah! It was good," Pallavi said.

"How about you?"

"It was okay. I missed 3 questions." I replied.

"That's okay. 12 out of 15 is a good score, buddy!" I knew I could have scored 15 out of 15 in that paper. Pallavi realised then she had to go. "Okay... You guys carry on. I have to go to the hostel."

"Okay!" I replied formally.

"See you then." Pallavi walked away.

"Yup. Bye!" I said, waving.

As she left, Pallavi asked Sanjana, "You are coming with us, right?"

"Yeah, sure! I will be there sharp at 5!" Pallavi nodded and left. I looked at my watch. It was 4:30 and I realized that I did not have much time.

"Let's go out. I will drop you till your hostel gate!" I told Sanjana so I could spend time with her.

"So, 15 out of 15?" I asked her about the test while taking steps with her.

"No Sam! I answered 14 of them!"

"Wow! That is good!"

"Actually, I knew 11 only. Then, I copied three from Pallavi." she said and giggled.

She looked pleased for those three extra answers copied from Pallavi than the 11 answers she solved. Girls feel a sense of accomplishment for small things - things that boys don't even bother about - like getting an extra mark in the exam, getting something free while grocery shopping, making the auto rickshaw driver agree on the fare they want, getting an extra pani puri after an argument with the Panipuriwaala... And, the most interesting part is that they always get excited when they find "SALE" written in bold.

"By the way, how come you got only 12? You were good with the concepts that day! I thought you will answer all of them."

"You know, the surprise test is bullshit!" I said, frustrated. "Who studies every day? Are we kids? I did not go through what he taught yesterday. There were three questions from yesterday's topic. And, none of my group mates had studied, else I could have copied from them."

"That's okay, Sam! This was a simple class test! Semester exams are the main exams! I am sure you will do well as you are good with the concepts!" I was better after her motivational discourse.

"So, what is the big plan at 5:00?" I asked.

"Oh…! We are going shopping and to have pani puri! Tomorrow Pallavi, Chitra and I are going window shopping, to the beauty parlour and lunch!" She was happy with her big weekend plans. I did not ask her to join me on an outing. I did not want to face any kind of rejection from her.

"That's great!" I replied. I noticed the difference of choice and mentality between boys and girls. Boys entertain themselves by playing and watching games, hanging out, boozing, watching action or triple X movies. Girls enjoy themselves with window shopping, being pampered in the beauty parlour, and indulging in gossip and chatting. That is why it is said – "Men are from Mars and Women are from Venus."

The cool breeze that blew created tranquility. The evening melted into night gently as we walked slowly on Maal Road. I observed her and wanted to be with her for some more time to savour the evening but sadly, we reached her hostel soon. We stood at the gate and she was ready to get in. "Hey Sam! Have you prepared the lab files for Monday's lab?" she asked.

"I haven't. But, I will do it on Sunday!"

"Oh... I don't have the readings and I don't know the steps for the last experiment."

"No problem. I will prepare it and give it to you tomorrow!"

"Thank you!" A cute smile spread on her face. I was waiting for it. "Okay, then. We will meet tomorrow!"

"Okay." I replied.

"Bye!" she said, waving her hand.

"Bye!" I said and kept looking at her like always. I left when she was out of my sight.

A long three-day-weekend had arrived. I had no specific plans. Some guys who stayed nearby were leaving for home. Some seniors were departing in local cabs for group outings. Everyone had plans except for me. "Shit yaar! What will I do these three days? These idiots should have made some plans!" I said to myself, abusing my group mates in disappointment. I reached the hostel and entered Bhaskar's room. Everybody was in a good mood – Bhaskar, Mrinal, Sanjeet, and Nishant were there.

"Aaiye! Aaiye! Everybody was waiting for you!" Bhaskar welcomed me.

"Great! Everybody looks like they are in the right mood." I replied.

"You came early today! Aaj Sanjana ne ghaas nahin daala kya?" Sanjeet taunted me and everybody laughed. I realized that they were in full mood today.

"Saale! Tujhe to aaj tak kisi ladki ne ghaas nahin daala hoga!" I replied and others laughed louder, except for Sanjeet.

"Anyway, leave all this and listen to the big news." Nishant said excitedly. I don't know why he was so involved. He was the most studious guy in our class.

"Mrinal is no longer single. He is committed now. Today, he proposed to Rashmi and she accepted!" Bhaskar said.

"Oh. Really? Awesome news, man!" I was excited. "Congratulations Mrinal!" I hugged him.

"Thanks yaar!" I saw real happiness on his face.

"That's why you didn't come to class today, right?" I asked, and he blushed in response.

"We will celebrate today for Mrinal!" Sanjeet stood up and said. "It's also a weekend, yaar!"

"Woo… Hoo…" Everybody was excited.

"Why can't we have a Daaru party tonight?" Sanjeet said. "Our first Daaru party. What do you say Guys?" Sanjeet was super excited but others were surprised with his new plan as nobody could think about it during the ragging period.

"Are you out of your mind?" Mrinal exclaimed. "We are still freshers. We can booze only after the Fresher's Party next Friday. We must wait till then."

"Huh… Fresher's party my foot! If today is the occasion, what's the point celebrating it next Friday?" Sanjeet argued.

"But, it should be feasible, right?" Mrinal had a logical point.

"Listen!" Sanjeet came close to tell us his trick as if it was a big secret. "I have an arrangement with one of the security guards at the main gate. We can bring alcohol in here. We don't need to plan for somewhere out of the campus!"

"Why take that much risk yaar?" We were surprised. "How can we do it in our rooms? Seniors may come to rag us at night!" I said, concerned.

"We can ask his roommate to lock the door from outside and if seniors ask, he can say that we had gone out tonight!" Bhaskar supported Sanjeet. He suggested the trick referring to my roommate as we knew that he would never be a guest for this kind of party.

"That's the idea!" Sanjeet thumped a fist on the table. "Our plan is ready. We just have to make the arrangements."

Nishant said, worried, "Guys, truly speaking. Meri to fat ke haath mein aa gayi hai. I have never drunk in my life. I think I should be out of this." He looked around, anxiously and said, "Are you sure it is safe?" It was expected from him. We knew him to be a sincere and studious guy, but he was always curious about our plans and activities. Some people don't know what they like. But the silver line is the "choice is always yours."

"If you are coming to the party, you will have to drink. Otherwise, you can be out of it!" Bhaskar admonished.

"Hey! Why are you so worried? Nothing will happen. Trust me. Just relax and enjoy the party!" Sanjeet placed an arm around his shoulders to pacify him. Now everybody, including Nishant was convinced and ready for the party. We felt excitement mixed with apprehension as it was our first "Daaru-Party" in college, that too during the ragging period.

Sanjeet divided the work for the arrangements. As expected, he took me with him to bring drinks from outside, like an assistant. Unsurprisingly, he showed his convincing and communicative skills everywhere and handled all complications with ease that a fresher could never have. He bribed the security guard in private to bring our party stuff inside.

"How did you sense that the guard would take the bribe? I could not have even dared to ask!" I asked.

"Hey kiddo! You don't know me. Once, I saw, a senior get clearance with the help of the same security guard. So, I used his name as a reference. And he agreed."

"Guys! We did it!" I said excitedly as we entered the room. They were impatiently waiting for us.

"Wow! Great yaar!" everybody praised us there.

"All credit goes to Sanjeet!" Mrinal said.

"Now everything is done – drinks, snacks and cold drinks!" Bhaskar said.

"The only thing left is to handle the seniors and get the door locked from outside!" Sanjeet said. "That can only be done by Sam. By the way, only he knows his roommate's mood swings and other secrets, right?" Everybody chuckled. They were enjoying and I left to convince my roommate.

I entered my room and saw him arranging his wardrobe. I stayed there for a couple of minutes, convinced him and then came back to the party room with him. Everybody welcomed and offered him a chance to stay, but he refused and before leaving, he locked the door from outside. Sanjeet, Mrinal, Bhaskar,

Nishant and I were inside the room and were ready for the party. Before starting, Bhaskar switched off the light, opened the windows and curtains and played light music. We had taken all measures to avoid being caught. Sanjeet had set up everything. We sat in a circle on the floor, with all the drinks and snacks in the centre. Everybody was excited to have their first drinks in college.

Our first shot was ready. All the glasses were raised in celebration. "Cheers to Mrinal! Cheers to our group!" We cheered and took our first shot.

"Yak!"

"Bhrrrrrrr!" Everybody made faces and funny voices after taking the first shot.

"How do people drink?" I thought, for it tasted bad. It was a secret that I had never drunk before and was drinking for the first time. I preferred not to tell them this. As our party progressed with the drinks, we started experiencing the after-drinking effect. With the room lights turned off, the dim soothing night light falling inside from the window, curtains waving in the breeze and soft light music playing inside, we gradually swung into a romantic mood.

"Wow! It seems like I am a romantic hero and am doing a ball dance with Miss Prerna, looking deeply into her eyes!" Bhaskar said.

"Oho! Romance is in the air!" Sanjeet said.

"This feeling is awesome!" Bhaskar said with his eyes closed.

"I know, I can understand bro!" Mrinal replied. "You know! Today when I proposed to her, she said that she had developed a liking for me from the very first day! I was completely overwhelmed! Now, I am madly in love with her, yaar!" Mrinal said, thinking of Rashmi.

Sanjeet, Nishant and I completed our first round of drinks.

"Har shaksh ki aankhon mein pyar hai,

Chalo koi to hai jo uska dildaar hai.

Hum bhi to khade hain line mein kabse,

Par saala kyon milta nahin koi yaar hai?"

Nishant recited a shaayari in between.

"Wah! Kya baat hai!" Bhaskar encouraged him.

"Kyonki tera har style puraana aur bekaar hai." I completed the shaayari and everybody laughed.

"Okay, boy! Tell us your story. Who is the lucky girl, you like?" Sanjeet pulled Nishant's leg, as he poured the second round of pegs into our glasses.

"There's nothing like that! You know, I am bullshit! I never had a girlfriend. And, I have never proposed to a girl! But, you guys are great! At least, you enjoy among yourselves!" With all the drinking, his speech was slurred.

"So what? You are good looking; everybody knows that you are studious and intelligent. You can get any girl you like!" Mrinal said.

"At least tell us, who do you like?" Sanjeet persisted.

"No, man! Leave it!" Nishant seemed shy. He took a moment and completed his drink in one shot and said, "Do you know Aditi from the Mechanical Department? She is the girl, yaar! Really! Beautiful!

I like her very much! But leave it. It's not my cup of tea." Suddenly, he stopped his emotional outflow as he realized that he wouldn't be able to get or impress her. But we were surprised when he revealed his crush on her as she was one of the most beautiful girls in college.

"Betaji! Khwab to bade unche unche hain tumhare!" Sanjeet replied. "But, that's okay. You have good rapport with most people in college."

"You should tell her your feelings. Who knows what there is in store for you?" Mrinal said. We signaled to him against it as he was drunk and not in his senses at the time. Mrinal winked at us and then said, "Come on! Call her and tell your feelings right now."

I stood up and pulled Mrinal away towards the wash basin. "What are you doing? If something goes wrong, we will be in trouble. Can't you see that he is not in the right condition? If she complains about it, then?" I warned Mrinal in a low voice. Bhaskar came to us and said, "He is right, you should not do this."

"Relax! I don't even have Aditi's number, neither has he!" Mrinal replied.

"We will connect the call to Preeti – that desperate girl!" Our jaws dropped in surprise as it was a big conspiracy. Preeti was an average girl but a real despo. She was interested in almost all the boys.

"Anyway he is not going to get Aditi. So, let have him try for Preeti!" Mrinal said. "Don't you think it will be an interesting pair?" He asked us with a cunning smile on his face.

"You are such a bastard. Why do you need to do all this?" I asked him with a serious expression.

He put a hand on my shoulder and said, "Life is too short bro! We should have fun always. Anyway, we are doing a good deed. We are match making, right?

"No! We are not doing it for match making, we are doing it for gaand masti!" I said. Mrinal just smiled.

"Guys, just do one thing - don't let him say Aditi's name while he talks to Preeti!" Mrinal instructed us.

Finally, we agreed and I whispered the plan to Sanjeet too. We started prepping Nishant to get ready to call.

"But, what if she refuses or gets angry?" After a lot of motivation from us, he was almost ready to talk. "And it's not the right time too, it's already 1:00 AM," he said with his eyes half open, looking at his watch.

"You don't have to worry about it. First, I will talk to her. If she is ready then you can talk. Okay?" Mrinal said.

"Okay. Let's do it!" Nishant said. "Hand it to me!" he asked for the phone.

"Wait! Wait!" Mrinal said and went aside to talk to Preeti. We don't know what he told her but he came back in sometime with a signal to get ready for the conversation.

"Hey Nishant! Start talking now. Aditi is on the line!" Bhaskar whispered in Nishant's ear.

The call was on speaker and Preeti started – "Is this Nishant?"

"Hi Aditi!" Nishant spoke and I put my hand quickly on the speaker when he said "Aditi", so that

Preeti could not hear the name. Nishant did not notice this.

"How are you?" Nishant asked.

"Yeah. I am good."

"Actually, I want to tell you something."

"Yeah Nishant. Tell me."

"I wanted to tell you that you are very beautiful. I like your smile very much. And you know, you look awesome in your blue dress. I notice you always." She did not speak a word but we could not hide our laughter. "I have liked you from the very first day of college. I… I think I am in love with you."

We grew silent when he said this.

"What are you saying Nishant?" She exclaimed.

"I am not asking you anything. I know I cannot match your standards. I just wanted to tell you my heart's tale," Nishant confessed, with a hand on his heart.

Everybody became serious after listening to his feelings for Aditi. We felt we had wronged him. He had the right to convey his emotions to his real love.

"That's all I had Ad…" I disconnected the call the moment he said Aditi's name.

"Very good. Congrats!" I appreciated him in order to hide the conspiracy.

"But, why did you disconnect? I wanted to hear her reaction!" Nishant asked, and his speech was slurred.

"Arre leave it yaar. Let her think about it. On Monday you can talk to her directly. Okay?" Sanjeet said.

"Okay, thank you guys for all this!" He said and collapsed on the floor. He was completely out. We finished another round of drinks with gossip on college trends and girls. We enjoyed our first party.

At around 3:00 AM Bhaskar slept off, Mrinal was sentimental with all the drinks going to his head and went to a corner of the room to talk to Rashmi on the phone. Sanjeet and I sat together.

"Come on! Let's have the last pegs. These idiots are gone now!" Sanjeet said and started pouring the drink in our glasses.

I took the drink and walked to the window. A feeble ray of light came from the bathroom door that was ajar. A silence prevailed inside the room with the light music reaching the ears faintly. "Tu jaane na…" the song, played on the system. Enhancing the effect of drinks, the breeze was gentle as I closed my eyes, looking outside the window, recalling Sanjana. The moments I had spent with her were flashing in my mind. I enjoyed being in love.

"Hey! What are you doing there?" Sanjeet asked. "Let me guess… Thinking about Sanjana, right?"

"You know, Sanjeet! I could not stop myself from liking her! She is one of the best things that happened to me. I feel elated these days, yaar!" I wanted to tell him my sentiments for Sanjana because I felt that there was bitterness in our friendship because of her. And, I did not want that to happen.

"It's good to see you happy buddy!" Sanjeet said with a smile. But, within a second, he changed his expression into a sincere one and said, "I would suggest you take things slowly. Take your time before you take a decision!" He put his hand on my shoulder and said, "Who knows!" We looked at each other purposely as we knew what he was indicating.

"Why are you saying this?" I asked him.

"As a close friend, I just wanted to remind you. That's all!" He said and went back to his place to avoid more discussion.

Sanjeet was always straightforward. But, today I felt that he wanted to convey something which I could not understand or, rather, I didn't want to. I enjoyed my moments with Sanjana. I called it a day and slept, thinking about Sanjana.

Chapter Seven

An evening at the Maal road

It was the first weekend of November. The sweet winter aroma started tingling in the atmosphere. The greenery on the mountains were more apparent now. You can enjoy the charm of Indian seasons closely if you live in a hilly area. The fresher's party was arranged by the seniors last month and the first year students enjoyed it to the fullest. We were free from ragging, completely. But this was the only college where the ragging period sustained so long. Now we had started feeling like a part of the college. We had become familiar with almost all faces here. Now it had become "Our College". Bhaskar and I sat on the stairs beside Maal Road one evening. Mrinal was busy with his girlfriend and Sanjeet was sleeping. We sat there for some time, watching couples and our classmates roaming around, gossiping and laughing.

"Life changes a lot," Bhaskar started. "Six months ago, I was preparing rigorously for exams and struggling for admission in a good college. I was busy with a different aspect of life, hard work, and tough competition. I landed up here and became friends with you guys and it gave me a new life. Then, I fell in love with her!" Describing all the changes in his life, he was now talking about Miss Prerna Rai. "I know I can't be with her. She is my teacher and older than me. Also, why would she love a loser?"

"There's nothing like that. Who said you are a loser?" I asked.

"Now the worst part is that she is leaving college in a week!" Bhaskar became emotional. She had already announced her goodbye in the last class. "You know, I proposed to her today?" he said without any enthusiasm.

"Wo…ho…! one sec… You proposed to Prerna Rai?" I almost yelled in excitement and he nodded. "Oh my god. You have guts man! I appreciate it! What happened then? What did she say?" I asked curiously.

"Nothing. It was an obvious "No" and then she gave me some gyan. You know how she is, right? She has a sweet heart. She told that she is getting married next month. She appreciated our friendship and suggested we maintain it for a lifetime. She said that I am a nice guy and can get a good girl in life."

"That's so true. Why are you depressed? You knew it was not going to work out and it had to come to this one day, right?" I said.

"Hmm… I know, yaar. But, love is so engaging that you don't want to look at the practical side. You just want to fly high with the feeling and don't want to let it go!"

"I can understand man. We are travelling on the same boat," I said with a smile there.

"I will really miss her elegant look with her sari, her irresistible classic charms. She appears like art to me."

"Wow man! I'm afraid you will become a writer in her memory. You speak like a poet. But, I am glad that you proposed to her. At least, you won't regret not doing it later. Why don't you just try your luck on that girl, Aakriti?" I tried to change his mood, indicating at one of the most famous and beautiful girls, Aakriti Rai. At that moment, she passed by us. "You like classic, right? She is classically hot."

He smiled. "See there! Sanjana is also roaming around. You can go if you want!"

"Leave it. Right now I am with you and she is with Pallavi," I refused.

"Anyway, what is going on these days?"

"It's the same. We talk in the lab where she is paired with me, but we talk less outside class. Twice we had study sessions and occasionally we take a walk together on Maal Road. Nowadays, she is busy with her new friends. But, we usually share texts every day. It's going on like a usual friendship," I said.

"So, why don't you drop a hint?" he suggested.

"Yaar! Truly speaking, this is not the right time. I am not sure if she likes me or not or whether she think about me that way at all. Let's give her some time."

"What if she gets engaged to someone else? You can't predict anything with girls. You know well the trends of the engineering college, right?" Bhaskar asked.

"In that case... nothing can be done. I don't want to make her my girlfriend; I want to make her my love. Let her feel the same way. I don't want to win a competition here! It's true that I like her very much. I expect her texts all the time; I eagerly wait for the lab sessions where we work together. I try to impress her with studies, with jokes and pranks. I am trying... I am trying my best... Let's see!"

"I admire your feelings and your efforts, bro!" he said, and patted my shoulder.

"Okay. Anyway. What do you think about apna hero, Mrinal?" He referred to Mrinal's love story and he wanted to know my opinion or rather, to confirm his opinion.

"He is enjoying his time with Rashmi. They make a good pair. What else?" I said in an obvious tone. "But, I genuinely feel like he is lost in his relationship. He is not able to define and differentiate between his life and love life."

"Exactly! That's what I feel too about him, too."

"It's like in just one month of his relationship with Rashmi, he is swiftly going away from us!"

"Yeah man! Most of the time he is not in the room. When he is in the room, he is either texting or on a call with her. And I am fed up of this "Baby" business - Baby, have you had your dinner? Baby, why are you sad? Baby are you okay?" Bhaskar looked frustrated and I could only laugh. "The most irritating thing is that when they go to their beds at night, they start talking on phone with their so called affectionate names like jaan, janu, baby, buddhu baby etcetera; it feels like they are not going to meet again ever and they talk with such intimacy. The next day, the first thing you find is that they are either talking on the phone or, roaming around together like every day! I personally don't understand this "do jism ek jaan" theory!" I chuckled at Bhaskar's description of Mrinal's love life. "I feel like there are lots of things happening around you, there are lots of people around you and you can be a part of it all and enjoy other aspects of life as well!" he said practically. "Occasionally, I taunt Mrinal and drop hints for him about this, but he says that I don't understand. I feel that he likes that life, or maybe he is so lost in his love life that he doesn't want to see the other aspects!" Bhaskar concluded.

"What I have realized is that Rashmi is juvenile and has a certain level of immaturity. Mrinal takes care of her at every step as he loves her very much. He is a responsible and loyal lover. I guess that is why he has changed. I think Rashmi is lucky to have him!" I said.

"Yes, you are right. Anyway, good for him. Good that he has got a beautiful girlfriend. I am glad for him."

"In our group, he is the most handsome and undoubtedly deserves to have a beautiful girlfriend."

"But, if this is love, then I am okay being single with my feelings!" Bhaskar said.

"There's nothing like that. It all depends on your fate, bro!" I contradicted his negative opinion. "Sometimes, it happens that you work hard to achieve something and you feel sad if you don't get it, but later you may realize that it was not meant for you. Conversely, sometimes you get something for free, and you don't respect and value it, but later that turned out to be the thing which you wanted exactly, but you hadn't realized it before." But yes, we should keep trying all the time. I am sure you will get a loving girlfriend in college," I said.

"See them! Nishant and Preeti!" I pointed at Nishant and Preeti, who stepped inside the academic block. "Who knew that a night's bluff call would change their life and they will be in relationship? All is well that ends well!"

"Han yaar! See them! They make a nice pair! Only they can tolerate each other."

"Seriously!" I supported his thought.

"Hmm…"

"I think we should go to our rooms now." After a long and exclusive conversation on our lives I wanted to wind that up.

"Yeah. Let's go," he agreed.

"We will play a round at room!" I said reminding him about the computer game we played in spare time.

"Okay. What about the upcoming exams?" he asked as we proceeded towards the hostel. "You know, from the 16th, the lab semesters are starting!"

"Arey. Don't worry. We'll manage," I said to pacify him. As dusk fell, we left Maal Road and headed towards the hostel discussing the exams. The evening-discussion made us halt for some time and take note of the changes happening in our lives.

Time flies when you are involved in serious business. In an engineering college there is nothing more serious than semester exams. Being freshers, the fear of the first semester exam made us study hard. Without getting involved in any other business, we studied earnestly, day and night. For the first time we experienced the potentiality of group study and it's results. We did well in the exams. We cleared the practical and theory papers without any difficulty. After the semester exams, we uselessly spent 24 days of the mid-semester break at home. We missed college and our friends badly and eagerly wanted to return to college. Occasionally, we communicated with each other on the phone and shared our experiences. Without anything significant done, we returned to college for the next semester with a new flavor and zeal in us.

Chapter Eight

The Contrast

"Shhh! Don't speak loudly Sam... This is library!" Sanjana said, as while explaining the concepts of "Basics of Electronics" in the library, unintentionally I spoke louder.

"Oh... I am sorry!" I said, realising that the librarian was also staring at me. This was the fourth time in my life I was coming to the library.

Since college reopened, the frequency of our meetings, calls and texts had increased considerably. It might have been because she got low grades in the first semester. With my efforts and combined study with our group mates and following the "Divide and Rule" policy amongst them, I was able to get "B" and above in all the subjects. That helped boosting my confidence and my hope of impressing her. With the increasing proximity with her, I could say that everything was working well too. "Can we go out now?" Sanjana asked in a low voice as soon as I completed the chapter.

"No! First, solve these three questions and then we will go out!" She frowned as I admonished her. I got assiduous and focused while teaching. She didn't disturb me with her out-of-context ideas and imaginative thoughts, although she wanted to. She interrupted when she had doubts. After the session, she switched to admonishing me.

"Do you know, there was a guy named Hitler Singh? Once he starts teaching, he thinks of himself as Hitler!" she whispered, taunting, looking at the question I asked her to solve. I chuckled at her. It sounded cute to me. I realized that she was getting friendlier and more comfortable with me, which was making me help her in her studies.

"We have only two days left for the sessional, right? And there is still one chapter left to cover!"

"Yeah. I know!" she said, and started solving the questions sincerely. I looked at her closely as she was making various expressions while solving the questions. That was my favorite time pass with her. After applying her intelligence and all concepts she had learned, she was able to solve one out of three.

"You know there is a famous saying – Bhusgol Vidyarthi ka bastaa bhaari!" I said and smiled. She took her notebook and hit me hard as soon as she realized that it was for her. The quote suited her as she had all the books and notes but wasn't able to apply or recall a simple formula and concept when asked to solve a question.

"By the way what is Bhusgol?" she asked.

"See! That's why I said Bhusgol! Without knowing the meaning too, you hit me!" She hit me again and I laughed.

"Bhusgol means intelligent!" This time, she pinched me hard as she realised that it was not the correct meaning. Then, we laughed for a minute. Then, I explained the rest of the questions. After the question-answer round, we wound up the session and came out of the library. This was our third session in the library after the semester break. I was pleased with progress on both sides. On the one hand, our intimacy increased with every session, and on the other hand, the syllabus was done before the exams. While walking down the stairs with me, she got a call on her phone and hurriedly answered saying, "Hey! I am going to my hostel. I will call you in 10 minutes."

"No. No. Carry on. You can go ahead and talk," I said, as I thought she disconnected it because of me.

"That's okay. By the way, if I am with Hitler Singh, can I disobey him?" she said, and we smiled.

We bid goodbye and left for our respective hostels. Thinking about the recent happenings on the way, I reached the hostel room. I entered the room and saw Sanjeet busy discussing something with Nishant. Bhaskar was transferring a movie in a pen drive while also talking about the movie to Rohit, who listened sincerely. Undisturbed by all the action, Mrinal slept with his mouth open. I entered inside and Sanjeet's concentration broke as he looked up at me.

"Aah! See, who has come. Our Superhero!" His taunt made everyone look at me and I gave them a silly smile. "Don't be mistaken guys. He is not an ordinary hero. He is a superhero in our group!" His taunt pinched me this time. I could sense that Sanjeet was jealous because of my increasing closeness with Sanjana. It was true that unlike before, I was participating less in group studies with them. But,

I was trying my best to balance both sides. "So, sir! How many lives you saved today?" he asked. "Oh I am sorry! The correct question for you is, how many chapters have you saved today for somebody?" he said. The others chuckled at his prank. Nishant and Rohit were also pulling my leg, and I felt it humiliated.

"Please give us also some tips, yaar!" Nishant said.

"Abe langoor, tughe angoor mil gaya na. Now keep quiet!" I said, referring to his growing intimacy with Preeti. Everyone laughed. Nishant shut up right then. With the noise and laughter, Mrinal woke up suddenly, and checked his phone for the missed messages and calls.

"See! Don't rub shoulders with our superhero!" Sanjeet joked. This time, I chose to keep quiet. And after some time, everybody resumed their activities. I changed my clothes, relaxed for some time and tried to join the others. Before the sessional exams, I participated and contributed to both sides' study sessions for the next two days. I devoted time equally with them to avoid misunderstandings.

Finally, the day arrived for which I participated in study sessions in many places with many people. After the last night's rigorous studying, somehow we woke up on time and got ready for the exam. We entered into the academic block to find our seating arrangements and amazed to see that there was a horde of students who were making a lot of noise while trying to find out their seating plan. It was published two days ago, but we were lazy. We made our way by pushing and jerking, till we reached the board to find our rooms and seats. This time, they had changed the arrangement from the last sessional. Previously, it was arranged according to the student's registration numbers, but this time, they switched it according to the class roll numbers. It was highly disappointing. Since the four of us had taken admissions consecutively during counseling, our registration numbers were in sequence. We sat together in sessional because of that. That was why we managed to get good marks in the internal exams. We were smart enough to fool the examiners and exchanged answers during the exams. Unfortunately, the arrangements were different this time.

"What the hell!" Bhaskar said.

"Shit, man! I was completely dependent on you for the second paper!" Sanjeet said to Bhaskar with disappointment. "I don't know! What I am going to do today?"

"Our strategy has failed this time!" Mrinal also added. "Hey guys! This is my class room. I am going! Don't worry. We will do well! All the best!" Mrinal said and left for his room. We wished him and stepped ahead to find our room. Bhaskar found his room. At the end, Sanjeet and I entered the same classroom because according to the roll numbers, we were almost adjacent. But, according to the new seating plan, Sanjana would be sitting between us.

"At least your wish is fulfilled!" Sanjeet said. "Enjoy!" he said, without looking at me, as if I had altered the arrangements. I couldn't find anything to say as a reply to that as I knew it was a big disadvantage for him.

"All the best!" I said. Without a reply he stepped ahead to have his seat at the last bench.

Sanjana sat in the second last bench. She smiled as she saw me. She looked happy with the arrangement as there was a possibility for her to get help from me. I smiled back. But I was concerned for Sanjeet. As soon as I sat down, the bell rang and the examiner distributed the question papers. Hurriedly, I went through it and was relieved to find that I could answer well.

The exam started and everybody had turned busy. In the first hour, I completed the questions I could answer. For the last half hour, I attempted the complicated ones. Sanjana poked me, asking to show her the answers. Undesirably, I had to indulge while simultaneously trying to answer the rest of the questions. Somehow, we finished our first exam. After discussing with Sanjeet and Sanjana about their papers individually, I tried to introduce the both of them to each other so that Sanjeet could get some help in the second exam after lunch, but he refused.

I knew why he was antagonistic towards Sanjana, but never imagined it was to this extent. I couldn't bridge the gap between them. My full concentration was on the exams. The situation continued for three days. We stuck to our usual routine i.e. studying, discussing and gossiping in our rooms. Thankfully, there was no serious gossip about my growing bond with Sanjana. I refrained from teaching Sanjana, except for occasionally explaining her doubts on the phone.

Somehow we passed the three days of exams without thinking about our performance. We were relaxed and stress-free on the third day, after the exam.

Sanjeet, Bhaskar and I met outside the academic block just after the last exam and the first thing Sanjeet said was, "Let's have drinks today."

"Okay!" I agreed though I wanted to relax at the room or chat with Sanjana. But I didn't want to refuse Sanjeet's ideas, otherwise he would tease me for it. Bhaskar smiled, which meant the plan was on. On our way out, Bhaskar called Mrinal to confirm if he was coming with us or not. "As predicted he is with Rashmi now and will join us in an hour!" After registering our names, we left the campus and decided to drink at "Cool-Joint", our regular boozing spot. Relaxed and indulging in some gossip, we reached our destination. Some other students had already reached there for a break after the exams. We expected it. This was a regular trend in college. We occupied our regular seats beside the window, where we could enjoy the fresh mountain breeze. It always added tranquility to the aftereffects of drinking. Bhaskar and I ordered our regular beers and Sanjeet ordered a hard drink for himself. It looked like he was in the mood today.

"Hmm... It looks like you were eagerly waiting for the exams to get over!" Bhaskar said to Sanjeet.

"Huh..." he said and laughed sarcastically.

"What happened? How was your last paper?" Bhaskar asked.

"I don't know what I have done in the exams this time. It was horrible. And this new seating arrangement screwed me. Anyway, leave this bull shit!" Our drinks were served as he replied in frustration. "But this arrangement has profited one person the most," he said after a pause and having the first sip of the drink. I understood that it was for me.

"And the award goes to Mr. Sam!" Bhaskar confirmed. Sanjeet laughed out loud, as if he was waiting for it. I could sense his differences with me because of Sanjana.

"Okay! Just tell me one thing, where was my involvement in the seating arrangement? Have I done anything?" I asked. "I tried to introduce him to Sanjana so that he could get help from her, but he refused because of his ego!"

"Wow! So many things happened and I don't even know!" Bhaskar drew in a big gulp of the beer.

"Do you think she would have shown me the answers?" Sanjeet asked.

"Why not? She is not like you think she is!" I said.

"That's what you think, you fool! Can't you see that she is taking advantage of you all the time? You don't even want to see how she is making a fool out of you!" Sanjeet said loudly. I was offended and it ignited a spark of anger in me.

"Okay... So you know what she is and how she is? Haven't you talked to a single girl in your life, you loser?" I asked, aggressively.

"Hey! Hey! What's going on?" Bhaskar interrupted. "Relax. We are not here to discuss on some silly topic and fight. Please change the topic. Let's enjoy our time here."

We didn't argue after Bhaskar's intervention but the argument sowed antagonism in my heart for Sanjeet. Bhaskar began speaking about other things to calm us down, but I couldn't participate fully as Sanjeet's comments lingered in my mind. By the time we completed our first round of drinks and the second one was running, Mrinal joined in.

"Sorry for joining late, Guys! By the way, which round is running right now?" Mrinal asked.

"Now the second round is over!" I said, finishing my drink and leaving the bottle on the table.

"Okay... But, why is the fun part missing here? Don't worry! Now, I am here!" Mrinal said. No one mentioned the argument.

"Hmm... Lagta hai aaj Rashmi se maar nahin khaya tu, isiliye itna josh mein hai!" Bhaskar made fun of him. We smiled.

Except for Mrinal, we had already started experiencing the effect of drinking. Despite it, we ordered the third round. The party proceeded with drinks, gossip and music. I participated with a smile, but my mind was full of thoughts. Why did Sanjeet hate Sanjana so much? Why did he think I was being fooled by her? Was he jealous? Was he old-fashioned?

The drinking session progressed to the fourth round with faster music and some dance moves. Mrinal and Bhaskar were in a good mood. Mrinal asked the bar manager to play his favourite tracks and encouraged the others to shake a leg with him. I was not up to joining them, although I always loved to dance. Mrinal insisted, but I refused.

"Leave him. He won't dance with us. Now he will only dance with his so-called friend!" Sanjeet tried to ridicule me. I don't know if it was the effect of three-

and-a-half bottles of beer or, if I lost my patience because I couldn't take it. I stood up with vengeance and pushed him. "What is your problem, haan? Why are you connecting me in every matter with her? Why are you so jealous?" I asked. Sanjeet and the others were amazed at my reaction. They paused for a moment and couldn't respond. The situation was tense. To avoid further conflict I left the joint. I started walking on the lane towards the hostel. Trailing me, Sanjeet and Mrinal stepped to reach me.

"Hey Sam! Listen," Sanjeet held my hand and I turned around.

"Why are you getting angry? It was a joke yaar," Mrinal tried to manage the situation.

"No. it was not a joke. It was intentional. Every time it cannot be a joke!" I yelled, as my anger was still not pacified. "Why do you think she is making me a fool? What was wrong if I taught her? What was wrong in my hanging out with her?" I asked, looking straight at Sanjeet. Sanjeet and Mrinal were listening to me in amazement. Bhaskar joined in right then. "Your chance of being my lab partner was snatched away. The seating arrangement was altered. You fear that I will not be able to spend time with you!" I said and Sanjeet's face bent down after my blaming.

"Why are you being selfish here?" Sanjeet walked away. Probably he was hurt.

"Hey Sanjeet!" Mrinal ran up to console him.

"What the hell Man! What you guys are doing? Fighting because of a girl!" Bhaskar shouted at me. "For god sake leave this topic! Let's move," Bhaskar pulled my hand and dragged me to the hostel.

Bhaskar and Mrinal tried to pacify me and Sanjeet and urged us not to discuss that topic again. The evening was spoiled completely and everybody reached the hostel. Without any further discussion, we went to our rooms. Later, I realized that the situation could have been handled differently. The damage was already done. The next day, I apologized to Sanjeet but it was accepted half-heartedly. I expected an apology from him but it didn't come. A shade of bitterness and distance came up in our relationship. We were talking and spending time in the group, but my bond with Sanjeet had vanished. On the other side, my intimacy with Sanjana resumed after the exams. We started meeting and spending time. What a contrast I was experiencing!

Chapter Nine

A day to remember

26th March, Saturday. The morning sky was clear and blue and the sun looked brighter. The atmosphere still bore the smooth winter aroma. This post-winter ambiance was common in a place like Sikkim. I had always admired the place for this. There is always moisture with sweet fragrance in the breeze. When you wake up in the morning and take a breath, you inhale the purest air.

All the surprises for the day started for Sanjana with a missed call. I left a missed call for a reason. She called back. I had changed my caller tune the previous night to "Happy Birthday" as a special treat for her birthday. After it rang fully, I picked up the call to wish her.

"Happy Birthday, dear! May your dreams come true! May you get all the happiness and comforts in life."

"Thanks You!... Thank You!" she said.

"Hey Birthday girl! Can you look outside your window?"

"Okay. But what is there?" No matter whether a girl likes a guy or not, she is always curious. And, guys can hardly realize that they are being noticed.

She looked out of the window to see a big balloon floating up on the boys hostel's terrace, with "Happy Birthday SANJANA" written on it. It was clearly visible from her hostel, as ours was about 300 meters distant from her hostel. "Wow!" she was dumbstruck. "I like it very much! Thank you!"

I saw her waving at me, for I was standing at my hostel's terrace to see her reaction. I saw her teeth when she smiled broadly.

"Why you did all these, buddhu?" The way she said "buddhu" was so sweet that I felt like kissing her. With her responses and our growing closeness, I really felt that today was the day to propose her.

"It hasn't even started dear! Be ready in an hour. We are going out!" I said.

"But, I had some other plans!" she said.

"I don't know about anything. You have to come with me!"

"Okay! I'll manage. But, where are we going?" she asked.

"It's a surprise Sanjana."

"Okay baba. I'll be ready in an hour!"

"Okay. See you at 10:30!" I cut the call. You can't execute big plans if you don't have enough money in hand. My pocket money couldn't manage the expensive arrangements I had made, and unlike every other time, I couldn't ask Sanjeet for the help. I borrowed some cash from my roommate and Bhaskar and got ready.

"Looking good, Sam!"

"Enjoy your day!" Bhaskar gave me a thumbs up, winking as I left. He was familiar with my plan for Sanjana. I winked in response and left saying, "Chal, Bye!"

It didn't take much time to see her coming out of the hostel in a magnificent outfit. I met her outside the girls' hostel. As she came closer, her light pink lipstick and eyeliner were more apparent. The fragrance of her perfume wafted. "Happy birthday, dear!" I wished her.

"Thanks!" She shook my hand with a smile on her face. "Now, can you please tell me where are we going?" she asked.

"Take a seat and enjoy your day. You are with me, so you can imagine how interesting it is going to be!"

"Oh… Achha… ! Let's see."

Chatting and walking slowly, we reached the main road in 10 minutes. I had planned a trip to Gangtok. Nobody could disturb us there. Gangtok was romantic and a beautiful place to spend time with your loved ones. It was the "love spot" for young couples. Usually, it took an hour to reach Gangtok using any conveyance from college. Generally, open jeeps or Sumos ran on a regular basis to Gangtok. Sanjana didn't know about my plan. We were waiting for the cabs.

"Let me guess. We are going to Gangtok, right?"

I shrugged. Since it was a holiday, local sharing cabs and jeeps were full. Finally, a crowded sumo stopped and the driver asked, looking at us, "Gangtok?"

"Haan, Bhaiya! Gangtok. But, there is no place inside?"

He got off to make the arrangements for us. He asked a local passenger to sit on the front seat with him. In a minute, he arranged for two seats in the middle row. He told Sanjana, "Aayiye madam."

I still looked at Sanjana to confirm, if she was comfortable.

"Let's go. Today it will be like this only!"

She pulled my hand to follow. I was happy - it was a good sign for all my plans to come. Sanjana sat by the window and I sat beside her. A fat man sat on the right, taking more than one person's space. It was good for me, because I was able to sit really close to her. Initially, I was hesitant to talk to her as we had not been in such close quarters before. A pure and gentle breeze blew. I could smell her perfume and the divine smell of her freshly washed hair mesmerized me. Her soft touch was creating a sensation in me that I couldn't describe. Without a single word, I relished those moments with her. 15 minutes of my full concentration was broken when she said, "Hey duffer! What are we going to do in Gangtok?" I don't know what made her call me "duffer", but it sounded soft and cute to me.

"Oh God! Save me today!" I mumbled to myself.

"What?"

"No. Nothing. I was saying, today you are going to experience things which you haven't before!"

"Okay!" she exclaimed. "How can you be so sure that I haven't experienced it before?"

"I just know, dear!" I said, looking at her. She stared back at me with her arched eyebrows. We weren't able to speak much during the ride as the driver had played some music. Over the 45 minutes long journey, we were engaged in experiencing the music, natural beauty and closeness between us. It was awesome! We reached the Gangtok Taxi Stand and got off. The weather was cooler now. The sun's rays were warm enough to balance the temperature.

"Come. Let's go!" I told her and started moving out of the stand.

"But where?" she asked as she caught up with me.

"Where else? M. G. Marg!"

We hopped up the stairs to cross the lane to reach M. G. Marg. In hilly areas like Gangtok, concrete stairs are built for pedestrians, connecting one road to another. It saves them from taking long, roundabout routes through the main road. We reached M. G. Marg. It shone with beauty. The high mountain ranges surrounded the space on all sides. Artificially beautified streets were filled with fountains, benches and flowers. Shops flanked both sides of the road. The setting was a perfect blend of natural and human art.

"It looks beautiful, today, hai na?" she asked to confirm.

"Maybe because it's your birthday!"

She frowned at me and then smiled gently.

"It is true!" I said, with a serious expression.

Busy window shopping, she walked with me on M. G. Marg. She wasn't aware of my plan. After passing a few shops, we reached Baker's Café. I suddenly turned into the shop and told her to come along.

"Arey… Why Baker's Café?" she asked. I didn't answer, but led her. When we entered, we saw a section of the cafe decorated. On the wall beside one table, it was written, "Happy Birthday, dear Sanjana! May you have all the happiness in the world. Have a blast today!"

"Arey! How do they know it's my birthday?" she asked.

"Yesterday, they called me and said that they knew it was your birthday and they wanted to give you a treat!"

She hit me hard on my arm. "Sam! It's wonderful. This is going to be one of my best birthdays! Thank you!"

"There is a lot more to come dear! I already told you, just enjoy your outing today!"

"But, don't you think it's too much? We could have simply come and have fun here!"

"What if the person is special for me?"

She sat down, while I went to the counter for the next arrangements. In a minute, I brought her favorite white forest cake in the shape of a teddy bear, with sparkling candles. According to my request, three of the café staff joined us for the celebration. Without wasting time, the candles were lit and she was ready to cut the cake with an elated smile. The staff started singing Happy Birthday. "Happy Birthday to you, Happy birthday to you, Happy birthday dear Sanjana… Happy birthday To… you…" It ended with all of us clapping. Some of the others who had come to the cafe had stood up and clapped, too. Sanjana blew the candles. She was happy and excited at the overwhelming welcome. She cut a piece of cake and came to me with it. I was nervous for a moment - this had never happened before. She fed me and smudged some cake on my cheeks, too! She giggled and said, "Thank you Sam!" I cut a big piece and fed her, and tried to smudge some cream on her face too.

"No… No… Please, Sam!" she insisted.

"Just a small one!" I tried to touch her cheeks as I didn't want to lose the opportunity. She agreed silently and I painted the cream gently on her soft cheeks. I fell in love again when I looked at her beauty, when she had her eyes closed.

"Happy now?" she asked in an all-knowing tone, and I couldn't say anything but smiled.

Sanjana offered pieces of cake to the people working there. She seemed happy doing that. I ordered some snacks and coffee to spend some more time with her. We sat unaccompanied there and she was smiling at me.

"Idiot!" she said, with a hint of affection. I never realized that "idiot" could sound so intimate and cute, too.

"What happened?" I asked.

"Nothing."

"Then?"

"You are one of the most entertaining and lively persons I have met so far!" She said it genuinely. It was a compliment. I smiled in response. Thinking about our relationship and the past few minutes, we were engaged subconsciously in observing the panoramic view outside, watching the waiters at work, occasionally stealing glances at each other.

To break the ice, she said, "Arey yaar! Semesters are starting from next month. I don't know! What will I do this time? And, labs are the most torturous!" she was clearly worried about the exams. I was listening, between sips of coffee.

"That's correct! But, don't worry! We will work something out for that!" I said. "We have a month to study! And today, no discussion on studies as it's a special day! It's all complete fun!" I said, to uplift her mood.

It worked well, as she smiled saying, "Okay, then! Actually, life should be like this! No need to study and just have fun all the time!"

"Definitely. Life is too short to fulfill all your desires. You know, my ultimate desire is to roam around all the beautiful places in the world and explore the varieties of lifestyles, foods and cultures!"

"Hmm… Hmm… And?" she asked.

"And, all this can be lovelier if I am with a good friend or someone special in life!"

To change the topic, she asked, "Where are we going after this?"

"We can go to Roll House, next!"

"Yes! Come on. Let's go!"

We left the Bakers Café, thanking the workers who made it special. We reached M. G. Marg again.

"We will sit here for some time. I love this place today!" Sanjana said, and sat on one of the wooden benches on the side of the road.

The roads were made of marble. The pavements were decorated with fountains and plants. It was beautiful and peaceful since vehicles were not allowed. We sat under the Vintage street lamp. A few people roamed around with their loved ones. The cool weather, hills on all sides, warm sunrays for a perfect balance and a beautiful girl you love sitting beside you: they were the perfect ingredients to make the day special. I thought about telling her my feelings, and was looking for the perfect moment. At the same time, I was hesitant, too. What if she didn't accept it and got annoyed? Then, I would not get to hang out with her. Caution was gamboling inside me. I was confident about my success too, because all the hints I had given her were received amiably. The mixed feelings were killing me.

"We had to go to Roll House, right?" I asked.

"Okay, sir! As you say!" About 20 lazy steps took us to the famous "Roll House". It was crowded as usual. "Roll House" is a small and beautiful shop at M.G. Marg. It was famous for its tasty rolls and momos. There was no space inside to sit, despite which crowds thronged for the mouth-watering dishes.

"What will you have?" I asked, intending to go in to place our order.

"One egg roll!"

I left Sanjana behind and went inside. I stood in the queue to place an order. There were already a couple of customers waiting. I reached the counter in five minutes and placed our order. "Bhaiya! One egg roll, and one plate momos." I paid for my order and waited to get it. I noticed Sanjana talking to someone on her phone. She became very serious. From her expressions and gestures, I realised that she was explaining or justifying something to someone. It worried me, as I wondered if everything was okay or not. She was busy with her conversation, not knowing that I was looking at her. As soon as our orders were ready, I picked up our food and reached her.

"So, what's the big deal, yaar? You are behaving like a kid!" I heard her yelling into the phone.

She turned around and saw me. Suddenly, her expression changed. She smiled at me, gesturing that she would take two more minutes to join me and started moving away from me as if she didn't want to have the conversation in my presence. For the very first time, her behaviour seemed strange to me. I sat on the bench and waited for her. With suspicion in mind, I waited for exactly seven minutes until she came back.

"Sorry Sam! It was my friend's call!" she sat beside me.

"What happened? You looked so tensed while on the call!"

"Nothing Sam! One of my school friends called me. She had an issue with her boyfriend. Leave it. Let's eat!"

She took a bite of the roll. I left the topic. Without any conversation, we finished our little meal, and I bought a bottle of water.

"Thanks for the roll and momos, Sam! It was awesome," she said. Without saying anything, I opened the bottle and gave it to her to drink. I staring at the movements in her delicate neck muscles while she was drinking water. I loved observing her mannerisms. It was 3:00 PM and it was the time to proceed to the next destination. Without wasting time, we got out of M. G. Marg, took a local taxi from the nearest stand to reach Namnang viewpoint.

"Ab to bata do! Why are we going to Namnang Road?" she asked. I just smiled.

"Are you kidnapping me?"

"How can I kidnap you in a local taxi?" I said. The ride was 15 minutes long. "We are about to reach, madam!" I said.

"Okay," she said. I paid the ride fare and we got off at Namnang.

"This is one of the best places to visit in Gangtok! It is called the Namnang viewpoint."

"Seems interesting!" she seemed excited to see the place. "You are my guide here?" she asked, amused.

"Anything for you, Ma'am!" I said, bowing my head slightly. She smiled at me. A passage led us to the viewpoint and it took all of a two minutes' walk.

"Oh my god! This is amazing!" she said, taking in the view. She took a few steps in a hurry to reach the edge, to enjoy the complete view.

"Yes. It is!" I said.

It really was amazing. Ahead of us, the natural scene of the hills with its dense greenery prevailed all over. On the right, there were intensely beautiful Kanchenjunga peak, capped with snow. The entire mountain range dazzled in the sunlight. It was the perfect season to be in Gangtok. The lower rightmost range was dotted with hillside houses on its slopes, as shops dotted the roadways of Gangtok. It was all perfectly arranged in a sloping sequence. Almost half the city was visible from there. Overall, it was incredibly natural.

"How come I didn't know about this place? It is awesome!" Sanjana was astounded.

We took a few minutes to soak in the exceptional beauty.

We sat at a secluded spot to gossip. "We can come to this place occasionally." I said intentionally.

"Haan yaar! It's a perfect place to visit! You have shown me such wonders today!" I smiled. We stayed silent for a minute.

"You know, a person should live his life in a place like this. You are away from dirty politics, crime, pollution and all the rubbish we experience in big cities!"

"Hmm…"

"The U.S – Iraq war, the Sensex crash, bomb blasts, onion and petrol price hikes – far away from all these things, this is a place to feel inner peace!"

"But these places are good only for vacations. Real life is in the metropolitan cities. Opportunities and growth are there in abundance!" she argued.

"That is a valid point. But it's a choice. People who stay here are compatible with this place. Some people like to live in these kind of places," I said and she nodded. "Okay then… After college, wherever we work, we will come to Gangtok once a year!" I said.

"Okay… But, do you think it is practical?" she asked.

"Why not? It depends on the intimacy and the level of friendship!"

"But where we will be, five years down the line?"

"Yes. I can see it. We work in the same company at the same place, probably Delhi or Mumbai. Everything is running smooth!"

"Hmm… Hmm…"

"We have a lot of fun. On weekends, we go for long rides in our car!"

"And, whose car is that? Yours or mine?"

"I told you na… Ours!"

She nudged me with her left arm. I pushed her back the same way.

"Arey! It is like, we have contributed and bought the car. That's it. And it can happen, right?" I asked. "We are freshers in the company. We share expenses. We share the same car. We share our time with each other!"

"Acha! And?" she hit me softly with mock anger. It seemed like the dream was acceptable to her. Her reaction made me confident about proposing to her.

"Sanjana!" I said, pushing her with a slight jerk by my right arm.

"What?" she asked, pushing me back again softly.

"You look beautiful. Especially, when you untie your hair. You know, I always watch you from the backbench in the class!" She was listening with a slight smile and a hint of pride on her face. Girls, especially beautiful ones, feel proud when they know that boys are attracted to their beauty.

"You are making me crazy, day by day! Sanjana…" I whispered, looking at her with warmth. When I was about to propose to her with the three magical words, a couple came there in search of a secluded spot, and they sat quite close to us. It was an abrupt interruption. Sanjana stood up, intending to leave. I assumed that she wanted to avoid the conversation. She had understood that I was about to propose to her.

"Hey! What happened?" I stood up and asked her as I didn't want to leave. Though she had shown some positive signs, I was unable to bear the suspense till I proposed to her.

"Nothing. Let's go." She stepped down and went to the edge for the complete view. I reached close behind her. I moved my face close to hers on the left side and pointed out ahead of us and said, "See! That is the Ranka Khola, at the bottom." She looked at the point, but was conscious of my increased closeness with her. She pushed me back slightly with her left elbow to show objection. After that, she smiled. I loved her girlish charms. When she realised I was not going to stop with my feelings, she turned around and stepped towards the exit. I followed her.

"At least inform me while leaving! I was telling you something, yaar!" I said, catching up with her and holding her wrist.

"I know that," she said with a faint smile.

"What do you know?"

She released her wrist with a jerk and started walking away with the same smile on her face. We walked on the stone stairs. Slanting rays of the sun fell on the ground, between the gaps in the leaves. Colourful flags from the monastery were strung everywhere. They were flapping in the gentle breeze.

The charms of nature and the feeling of love made it an unforgettable affair.

"Wait. I want to take you somewhere!" I said excitedly.

"I think we should go back to college now," she said observing my enthusiasm, but I was sure she didn't mean it.

"Half of the movie is left dear. I asked you for time for the whole day!" I said and giggled. "Come!" This time I extended my hand and she held it. I made regular progress on my way to impress her. According to my plan, I took her to the Ropeway Center for a ride.

"Oh! Ropeway ride!" she said, unsuccessfully trying to hide her excitement.

"It will be a great fun. Have you ever been on the ride?"

"No." It was expected from her. And that was why I had planned it.

"Could you wait here, madam? I will make arrangements and come back in a minute!" She nodded and I left. I booked an entire box to have our privacy. They arranged it for me. Everything was perfect.

"Let's go!" I came back and took her to the entrance of the Ropeway Ride, where we were asked to wait for five minutes. Chairs were arranged in a queue for the waiting passengers. We sat behind five people in the queue.

"You are completely different today, Sam."

"Do you like this Sam or, that Sam?" I asked, though I could read a hidden fondness for this Sam in her expressions.

"Definitely, that Sam!" she said. "That Sam was sweet and was my friend!"

"And how is this Sam?" I asked but she didn't reply. I didn't ask again and we were silent for some time. I was thrilled by today's happenings and the love inside me. In a couple of minutes, the gate keeper yelled at us, "It's your turn, Sir!" I stood up as I heard him. "Let's go!"

"It's all yours, sir!" the gatekeeper said, looking at us.

"Only the two of us will be in the box?" she asked as we entered and the gate was about to close.

"Yes! It's all ours!" I replied.

"You booked the entire box?" She was surprised. I could not answer her. The box started moving on the rope. "Why are you spending so much, Sam? We could have enjoyed by sharing, too." I was glad that instead of worrying about our complete privacy in the box, she was concerned about the expenditure.

"That's okay, dear. I want to spend this special time with you! You are important for me, not money," I said affectionately. She couldn't reply after that. The box moved on, slowly rising in speed. She looked through the glass at the panoramic view outside. "Wow! We are completely airborne Sam! See there, at the bottom!" she pointed at something.

I leaned in close, making physical contact from her back as she looked outside. I put my hand around her waist and moved my face close to hers. She was nervous when she felt my touch. My right hand slipped on her belly, winding around her waist. My face rested on her shoulders and my rough cheek was touching her soft one. We experienced an affectionate proximity. Without saying anything, I sensed that she was completely thrilled. Her heart was beating fast.

"Hey Sanjana!" I whispered in her ears.

"Hmm."

"You didn't answer my question?"

"Which question?" she was hardly able to speak.

"How do you like this Sam?" I whispered and turned her around gently towards me, without disturbing our closeness. I lifted her face with my left hand and pulled her closer with my right hand. She let me do it amiably. I stared at her from up close. She was stunning. A sensation ran all over me. For the first time, I was going to kiss a girl. Indicatively, I had her consent too. Finally, I touched her lips, I felt them. I kissed them. I kissed her soft, delicate lips. I embraced her and kissed her deeply. She wasn't participating at first, but submitted herself to me. We were lost. That moment was inked in my memory for a lifetime. I was exhilarated to have my first kiss in mid-air! We were surrounded by mountains and dense clouds. It was perfectly romantic. I held her tight, kissed her and caressed her for a couple of minutes. My testosterone was aroused as I experienced her curves closely. We came back to our senses when her phone vibrated, signalling the arrival of a message. We separated as she took out her phone to read the text. I was completely mesmerized by my first kiss. I stared at her with tenderness while she was busy replying to the text.

"Hey!" I held her by her waist. She kept her phone inside after replying. This time, she tried to release herself by slightly pushing me with her hand on my chest.

"We should not do this, Sam!" she said but, I didn't let her free.

"Hey, Sanjana! Listen! I love you. I love you very much." Finally, I had proposed. "You are the best thing that has happened to me! Now show me your cute smile, once!" I said, and this brought a really cute smile on her face. As soon as I realized that our ropeway ride was going to end, I took advantage and kissed her one more time. She couldn't oppose as I kissed her again with the same passion.

"Hey! We are about to reach!" she reminded, breaking away. We disembarked from the box as we reached Deorali Ropeway stand. The security personnel were guiding passengers to a safe exit. It was evening already, and dusk had fallen. A few steps took us out of the place onto the main road. The evening chill had set, giving us light shivers.

"It's a bit cold here, Sam!" she said, shrinking inwardly, with her arms crossed.

"Yes, it is. Should I buy you a sweater or jacket?"

"I know you are good at these things. But don't be so generous! It's fine for now. I already have a lot of warm clothes in my room. I just forgot to bring some along!" she said. "But, what next? Aren't we going to college now?" she asked, expecting we would be leaving now. I smiled at her, saying nothing.

"What? Is there more left?" she enquired.

"Yes. Dinner!"

"No, Sam! It will be very late if we wait till dinner. Its 6:15 now. I told Pallavi that I would have dinner with her!"

"But, I have already planned it!" I said.

"Okay. I will manage, somehow!"

"Don't worry! You are completely safe with me!" I said, placing my arm around her shoulder as we started walking on the street. After today's incidents, I was confident at the thought of being close to her.

"Hey! It's a public place, Sam!"

"That's okay! Itna chalta hai yaar!" I said and removed my hand to make her feel comfortable.

"What is that?" Is there a road show?" Sanjana asked as we saw about 30 people gathered by the roadside ahead. We went closer and saw that it was a tea stall.

"So, it's a tea stall. But, why it is so crowded?" she asked.

"The famous Darjeeling tea is available here!" I guessed as I read the shop name on the board above: "Darjeeling Tea Stall".

"Let's have some! I have never experienced Nukkad tea before. I have heard that it tastes good!" I couldn't refuse. I ordered two teas as soon as we reached. In a minute, we were served two hot teas in white clay cups accompanied with traditional plates. A childlike excitement flared on her face. She smiled, looking up at me. She looked around and saw people sipping tea from their plates instead of using their cups.

"Hey! What are you doing?" I asked when I saw her pouring tea onto the saucer. She smiled momentarily and concentrated on her tea. She looked like a child, sipping from the plate. After every sip, the breath she exhaled was filled with steam. I looked greedily at her, with my mouth open. I was sure, at that moment, that she was the one I wanted to spend my whole life with. It is the sweet effect of love that the person you love appears exceedingly beautiful, cute and lovable to you in all that they do. "It was good na?" she asked after finishing her tea.

"What?" I asked, pretending as though I had no idea what she meant.

"Tea!"

"Oh! I thought..." I said and smiled shrewdly as though I was thinking about our kisses. I stood up, thinking she might hit me for it.

"You! Sam ke bachhe!" she ran after me for fun on the pavement. She never looked as natural and free as she was that day. She had faith in me. I was falling deeper and deeper in love with her.

"But, it was awesome!" I said genuinely and she hit me on my arm with a shy smile. We walked some more, chatting lightly. "Now where are we going for dinner? It's already 7:30 and I have to reach hostel on time!" she said.

"A 10 to 12 minute walk with me will lead you to the famous restaurant, "The Cuisine" and you can have me and the delicious dishes for dinner!" I joked. I loved to see her smile and to hear her laugh. That was the Sanjana I loved. With the flourescent streetlights illuminating us and vehicles sounding off their horns on the street, we had a romantic walk on the pavement.

"You didn't tell me how your day was. Did you like it?" I asked.

"It was awesome. I hadn't thought this much could happen in a day!"

"And what about me?" I asked, to confirm our relationship.

"What about you? You are an idiot!" she said and laughed. I couldn't understand her reaction, but realized that this might be one of those girlish expressions I hadn't experienced before.

"Hey! We've reached the restaurant!" I said. We crossed the road to reach it.

"Just wait, I will join you back in two minutes. I am going to confirm our reservation." Without waiting for her reply, I went inside. I confirmed the special arrangements I had made at the reception. When I came out, I could not find her. I stepped out ahead on the pavement and found that she was walking and talking on the phone.

"She talks on the phone all the time!" I muttered to myself. Unaware of me, she was busy on the call, wearing a serious and disappointed expression on her face, as if she was being yelled at on the other end.

"But why? What is the issue?" she yelled. I was amazed at her reaction. She turned around, unaware of my presence and was shocked to see me. She put up a fake smile for me. I could sense that she was disturbed with the conversation.

"Okay… I am going for dinner now. Bye!" She cut the call as if it was intentional, because of my presence.

"Hey! Hey! That's fine. Finish your conversation!" I said, with a suspicion tingling in my mind. Without responding, she began walking towards the restaurant. I held her wrist to stop her. "What happened, dear? Any problem?" I pulled her slightly towards myself. "Hey! You can tell me any of your problems, issues. Or anything… I will always be there for you!" I said, holding her hands and looking straight into her eyes. She held her head high and looked at me. "I don't know, Sam," she said. There was no difference in her annoyance after my intervention.

"Anyway… let's go… Everything is fine," she said, releasing her hand from my grip.

"But, why can't you tell me?" I asked.

"Because there's nothing to say, Sam!" she yelled. "Let's go for dinner." She pulled me by my hand and tried to ease the situation as she realized that I was upset. Without a word, I walked with her. A hint of suspicion started roaming about in my thoughts. Why was she so resistant to tell me anything?

At the restaurant, the usher let us in. The beautiful ambience of "The Cuisine" calmed us down. We entered and headed towards the reserved table, guided by the well-dressed waiters there. We were welcomed with such warmth that we forgot our argument. Fresh roses creating the perfect romantic setting. Dim lights and ancient sculptures on the wall created a soothing sight. The soft instrumental music made the environment tranquil. The chairs were drawn for us and we sat down. Almost immediately, two violin players came up to our table and greeted Sanjana. "Happy Birthday Ma'am!" They started playing the Happy Birthday song on their violins.

"Wow!" She couldn't stop herself. I never imagined before that a birthday theme could be played this well on a violin. It was amazing. I chose to book a reservation there because of the hospitality and ambience. I was proud that I had brought my first girlfriend to such a place for dinner for her birthday.

"I really don't know what to say today!" she held my hand and said as the music ended. Menus were brought to us. "I've never had such a special birthday in my life. It was an awesome experience today. You are changing my life swiftly and sweetly, Sam! I love it!" she said, looking at me affectionately. It gave me a sense of pride that all my plans were successful. Now I could tell my friends proudly that I was not single anymore. "But, how come you haven't had a girlfriend before? You are very romantic!" she asked.

"I studied in a boy's school, and like in many traditional boys' schools, boys are sloppy and rough. Nobody speaks a sentence without slang and the gossip about girls is hyped and exaggerated, which makes them uncomfortable about being acquaintance with girls at that age. I had a big gang. We used to have fun always! But, gradually, I am getting friendly and comfortable with girls!"

"Hmm... So now, this is the real Sam, right?" she asked, after she heard my story. I just smiled in reply.

"Hey! Come on, now, order something you would like!" I said, changing the topic and handing over the menu to her. She had a look at the menu, and finally decided to order. "Two hot and sour soups, one Sabji Jalfrezi, one Chicken Nawabi, three Butter Naans."

After she ordered, she stood up and said, "I am going to the washroom. I'll be back in a couple of minutes!"

She left her phone and purse behind. I looked around with a sense of achievement and happiness: I was no longer single! My friends would tease me for good measure, now. I would have to throw a party for them and I was already bankrupt after today's expensive treats. But the only thing going on in my mind was that everything is fair in love and war. Most importantly, I was ecstatic about my new relationship.

The only thing that made me dejected were my differences with Sanjeet. I couldn't understand why he hated her so much and why all this happened between us. Brimming with positive energy, I thought I would sort out the issue when I would return to the hostel. Just then, her phone vibrated and flashed half a message from a sender saved as "Dg". The screen was locked, so only this much was visible: "I'm sorry Jaan!" A sudden suspicion filled my mind. I took her phone to read the text message. I knew the combination to unlock it though she never told me. I had noticed it before. The message I read stunned me. "I'm sorry Jaan! Us kabooter se door rehna and try to reach hostel on time. Love you..."

My eyes were glazing over. My heartbeat stopped and mind was blocked. I couldn't comprehend anything. "Kabooter" was definitely meant for me. None of her female friends would use "Jaan" and "Love you" in their texts. I tried to confirm with other messages in her phone, from the contact saved as "Dg". It was clear that those special words were used in almost every message. They were in a relationship.

I was traumatised. I couldn't understand how to react. Should I be angry at her betrayal? Should I feel sad that my love didn't succeed? Should I feel frustrated at my luck? Should I repent wasting my time and emotions on her? And yet, still, a thin ray of hope sought existence in my mind, which forced me to call "Dg" from her phone. It rang and my heart beat fast. I desperately wanted to hear the voice on the other end. After a few rings, a male voice spoke, "Hello Baby! I knew you would call me. Where are you? You reached your hostel or, you are still with that kabooter?"

Without saying a word, I disconnected the call. I was betrayed, cheated and fooled. I was broken. I nearly threw her phone on the table and sat brooding. Sanjana came back without the slightest hint of what had happened in her absence. Her phone vibrated again. Probably "Dg" had called back. Without a word to me, she answered the call. "Hello!" She paused for a while and then said, "Yeah! It was disconnected because of a network issue. Will call you back later!" The conversation had ended. She realised that I was the one who had called him.

She stood speechless. She knew that I had figured out the twist and was raging. I was now seeing a shrewd and intelligent betrayer. My mind was not accepting it at all. I looked at her furiously. She didn't dare to look at me.

"Who is Dg?" I asked.

Looking down, she was quiet. It proved the worst to be true.

"What is this Sanjana? Who is this Dg?" I yelled. "For god's sake, say something!" I wanted to listen to it from her. I wanted her to tell me that whatever I had come to know of was not real. But, sadly, there was no reply from her. Workers began noticing us.

"Sam... I was about to tell you," she said, frightened.

"When? After using me completely?" I yelled. "I can't accept this. Please tell me that there is nothing like this!" I took a step towards her. My eyes brimmed with tears. "Those moments, that friendship, that love... It was all fake, hai na?" I said in a brittle voice. I stared at her, disappointed. I noticed that she was crying. She began weeping bitterly.

"I am... Sorry!" She was hardly able to speak. Tears poured from her eyes. Nothing pacified me. I was broken within.

"But remember one thing. My love for you was true. I loved you! I loved you from the bottom of my heart!" I said with moist eyes.

I left her in a fury towards the counter. At the counter, I asked for the bill. With a professional smile, they calculated the rate and gave me the bill in a minute. They may have guessed that we were fighting. I didn't care. I just paid up and returned to her. She sobbed with her head down on the table.

"I am leaving," I said. Her sobbing increased. She lifted her head and I saw her teary eyes.

"Plea....se...". she said. It didn't do anything for me. I left the restaurant in fury and started walking on the streets of Gangtok, leaving her behind. The sound of horns and flashing headlights from vehicles running on the road, the sound of people walking on the streets and the moderately chill air didn't affect my senses in any way. I walked aimlessly. I was not able to believe this sudden turnaround. I didn't realize how long I had walked, and slowly began to tire. I couldn't stop myself, despite the fatigue and kept on walking, recalling the past. I tried to deduce the reason. Why did she never discuss her past relationship with me? I was broken. I didn't notice where I was walking.

When I was completely tired of walking, I stopped. I noticed a secluded spot. It had no streetlights and there was no one. I reached a desolate shop around the space. I sat in front of the closed shop on the stairs and leaned back on its shutter. The memory of my love story; from the first meeting till today's celebrations, the kisses and the heartbreak – all of it ran in front of my eyes. I couldn't stop my emotions from getting out. I burst into tears. I didn't know how long I sat there. I came back to my senses when my phone rang for Sanjana's call, and I found that there were many missed calls from her which I didn't realize while walking. I disconnected it as I didn't want to talk to her. She knew I wouldn't answer her call, so she texted me saying, "Where r u Sam? r u alrite? Please. please reply. I am sorry..."

I gathered my wits. I decided to reply, thinking that it was 9:00 PM and she was alone in the big city. It was my responsibility to make her reach the hostel safely. "A cab driver will call u for the pickup. Tell him ur location. He will drop u at girl's hostel safely."

I had already booked a cab in the morning. To confirm the ride, I called the driver and gave him Sanjana's number. I gave him strict instructions to drop her at the gates of the girl's hostel. I was not in a state of mind to go to the hostel and face my friends, especially Sanjeet. He always wanted Sanjana out of my life. I couldn't understand why. I recollected the arguments and repented. I fought with him without listening to his point. In the end, I lost my friend. I lost my girlfriend. I lost myself. I lost everything. Again, I had a message from her.

"Please come… I won't go without u. Please… Please."

I didn't reply. I smiled sarcastically, looking at her text. I knew that she would wait for some time and then leave, as the girl's hostel warden was strict. They had a daily attendance rule at 10:00 PM and she couldn't risk it. My thoughts drifted towards my hostel. I realised that everyone would be in the mood to celebrate – it was Mrinal's birthday the next day. I couldn't handle it in this mental state. I texted Bhaskar saying, *"Hey bhasu! I will nt be able to come today. I will be there by 2morrow morning. Please manage there na…"*

I switched off my phone as I wanted to be alone.

I had made up my mind not to go to college. I walked inadvertently on the side of the highway. I reached a cigarette and tea shop, and bought a cup of tea and a packet of cigarettes. I sat on a bench by the shop, noticing the hard core labourers drinking tea and smoking beside me. Night transport trucks had started running on the highway. It was around 10:00 PM. Lost in thought, I sat sipping my tea and smoking. I was sad and alone.

After sometime, I left the place and wandered around on the streets of Gangtok with a sense of loneliness. I started walking towards M. G. Marg. Only a shop or two were open there. The streetlights and the grey-marbled road were prominent without the shop lights distracting from it. A couple of people were roaming about. I crossed the street, the roll house, the benches - and noted the marked contrast in the space with the mornings.

For no reason, I walked up to Namnang View. I crossed the desolate and dimly-lit path, and reached the point where we had some time together. I experienced the same mountain ranges and natural beauty with a different perspective now. The mountains, the moon light and the cold air deepened my grief. Far ahead, the snow-capped Kanchenjunga ranges dazzled in the moonlight. I sat alone, with a cigarette in hand. It was the same place where we had some romantic moments, just a few hours ago.

What a day it was! I hadn't imagined in the wildest of my dreams *that this much could happen in a day. Starting with impressing her by setting a Happy Birthday hello-tune and flaunting the balloon from* the *boys' hostel terrace, then her* birthday *celebration* at *Baker's Café,* and then experiencing the *charming viewpoint and the ropeway ride, my first kiss, - and then everything vanished. Why* was *I chosen for this? Why did* she do *this to me?* Despite *my love for her*! *With moist* eyes, a cigarette in hand and staring up at the mountains, I wondered to myself.

Jo hanste hue chalne ko saath aate hain,
kuch door tak wo chal ke laut jaate hain.
Ab to ho gaye hain hum akele aur tanha,
ki unki bewafaai ki gajhal hum gaate hain.
Jab apno ko bhi gairon mein ginaana tha,
to do wakt ka ye pyar kyon jataate hain.
Har rang mein bhi rang ke berang kar gaye,
ab rang bewafaai hum pehchaan jaate hain.
hai har taraf se bewafaai ne mujhe ghera,
ab bewafa ko hum wafa se hi haraate hain.
Jab wakt hi us wakt se paaband ho chala,
har wakt ko us wakt se milaate hain.
Abhi tak door se hi chaand humne dekha tha,
ab to chaand mein bhi daag nazar aate hain.

Chapter Ten

My Lonely Days

I reached hostel in the morning. Everybody, including Sanjana, was worried about me. I refrained from any conversation with her. I manipulated my friends about my stay at Gangtok. I didn't want the story of my heartbreak to become public yet. Genuinely, the twist left a huge impact on me. I became serious and began participating less in fun activities in the group. I began roaming alone. I savored my memories and smoked frequently. My interest in class and in my studies vanished despite knowing that the semester exams were just around the corner.

With the changes in me, I noticed some changes in Sanjana, too. She had transformed into a serious and sad Sanjana from a jovial one. She refrained from active participation in class. She observed me closely and regularly, trying to talk to me. I declined responding each time. I couldn't bring myself to talk to her. Whenever I saw her, I felt betrayed and cheated. It instigated more hatred in me, towards her.

My friends kept asking about my changed behavior and uncouth appearance. I made excuses of not feeling well and, initially, they accepted what I said and didn't question it. Despite my differences with Sanjeet, he came to my room twice to ask after my well-being and health. It roused my guilt more. These emotions and thoughts restricted me from indulging in active participation in everything that was happening around. On one of the evenings when I sat alone in my room, Sanjeet and Bhaskar entered with a bang. Sanjeet took a look at me and my room and yelled, "Hey, Romeo! What do you think of yourself? You can bluff others, but not me! I know what has happened and why you are so isolated these days!"

Though he was yelling at me, his care was apparent. I understood him well. He took a moment and said – "What kind of friend are you? Couldn't you tell us this?" I don't know why, but his words touched me and I began to cry. All my suppressed emotions escaped finally.

"I am sorry, buddy! I am really sorry! I fought with you for that bitch!" I said, crying. He embraced and patted my shoulder.

"That's okay! We are friends!" he said, with warmth in his voice. His anger was gone. It gave me emotional relief. I didn't have the courage to face him with the guilt of what I had done.

"Hey! It's okay! Shit happens, yaar!" Bhaskar said, patting my shoulder. We settled in a minute and lit up cigarettes.

"But, you should have told us yourself, man!" Sanjeet said.

"I thought…" I began, when Sanjeet cut in.

"I thought what? You idiot!" His care was evident and it moved me.

"Now tell us the whole story. What happened that day?" Bhaskar asked as he exhaled a puff of smoke.

"First of all you tell me, from where did you get to know something happened?" I asked. Impulsively, Sanjeet and Bhaskar smiled at each other. "What? What are you smiling at?" I asked curiously.

"We didn't hear anything. We just guessed. Bhaskar told me that you and Sanjana went to Gangtok and it was after that, that you became Devdas," Sanjeet said. "When I noticed this inertia and dullness in Sanjana, too, I was sure that there was something wrong between the two of you!" Sanjeet was proud of his intelligence. I was amazed at the same. I was relieved at talking to them after a long time.

"Have you ever seen a real bastard?" I asked Bhaskar. He smiled at my jocular reference to Sanjeet.

"He is the one." I said, pointing at Sanjeet. We shared a laugh. That evening, I spoke a lot after a long time. I told them that day's events. They heard it, unblinkingly. Bhaskar was very interested in the romantic part. Sanjeet was serious when he heard about the break-up. After I finished, they did not say a word for a moment. It seemed like they were swept away with my love story. After some time spent in silence, Sanjeet spoke up. "See! I told you that day, right? My observation and prediction can't be incorrect! But don't worry; I will arrange for a setting with him. He doesn't know me!" Sanjeet was furious at the deception and wanted to take revenge on her boyfriend. "Just wait and watch!" Sanjeet said, as he stood up.

"Hey! Hey! Calm down. It's over now!" I tried to pacify him. "Leave it. By the way, if that girl is not genuine, if she is not mine… what's the point doing all these things?" I said. I turned quiet for a moment, realizing the reality of what I had just said.

"In the entire story, one thing was interesting. You had your first kiss here, right Sanjeet?" Bhaskar changed the topic.

"Yes. But, it was too expensive yaar!" Sanjeet said and they laughed aloud. I was smiling, too. Though there was nothing that could erase Sanjana's memories from my mind, that night I tried to get involved with them in the gossip and felt relieved. I enjoyed their company after a long time. It made me feel like I was not alone. It filled me with emotional strength and confidence. We missed Mrinal a lot, but like always, he was busy with Rashmi.

"You remember our first ragging incident? When Mrinal and I were caught smoking in the corridor by the seniors?" Bhaskar asked, smiling widely. He was lost in the memory.

"I joined you later!" I reminded him.

"As usual this idiot escaped!" I pointed at Sanjeet, wearing an envious expression.

"I am not like you, you idiots! I have my tricks and connections for every situation!" Sanjeet said.

"Did you know, that day, Mrinal argued with seniors for me!" Bhaskar said his gratitude obvious. "He almost fought with them!" Bhaskar said. His love and sense of friendship for Mrinal was evident.

"He did!" I agreed, recalling that incident.

Taking a moment and heaving a sigh, Bhaskar said, "Now, this guy has changed completely. In class, he sits with Rashmi, after class he spends time with her, and at night, he is busy on the phone with her. He doesn't have time on weekends either, for us! I feel like I don't have a roommate!"

Mrinal was madly in love with Rashmi. He didn't realize that he was swiftly isolating himself from us. "You know, two days ago, he was tensed because of his argument with the locals. They teased him and Rashmi, and he argued with them badly." Sanjeet said.

"The problem is that Rashmi is a local. Aur unki jhaant jali padi hai ki how come he has got a beautiful local girl as his girlfriend!" Bhaskar said, angry at the locals.

"Yes. That is true," Sanjeet said.

"Oh! I didn't know this!" I said, surprised. I was not aware of his recent dissension with the locals.

"If it goes again, I will tell Sabu sir." Whenever Sanjeet was in trouble, he went to Sabu sir. "By the way, how can you know? These days, you were also away from us, pretending to be another Devdas!" he taunted me.

"I am sorry guys!" I said. "In my attachment with her, i was completely lost. But you know, I am still not able to believe what she did to me! Every time I recall the past and try to find if there was any authenticity in it or not! Was anything real, or, was everything fake? I am unable to find an answer. This disturbs me all the time," I said with a sigh.

"You had a lot of emotional investment in her," Bhaskar said. "It will take time. Time heals everything!"

We ended the conversation in the next few minutes. It was already 3:00 PM and we had had a continuous gossip session for six hours! That night, we slept in the same room, joining two beds together. I slept well that night, after a long time. It took me a few more days to recover partially from the emotional trauma. Sanjeet and Bhaskar helped me. They tried to be with me most of the time, enjoying, commenting, gossiping and involving me in fun activities in class. They made me participate with them. Occasionally, Mrinal and Nishant joined us for fun. But, they were caught up in their own world. With time, I noticed a behavioral transformation in Sanjana, too. She was less considerate about her appearance and charm which made her look genuine and naturally beautiful. In class, she shrank from the amusement and gossip with her classmates and began concentrating on her studies.

With the unsolicited changes in the past month, she tried to settle things down by texting me saying sorry. She would, on occasion, ask after my wellbeing and trying to talk to me. I couldn't bring myself to respond to her requests. After 40 days from that special day, I broke out of my silence and stubbornness and finally replied to one of her messages.

"I am fine now. Good to see u studying in class. Carry on... Bye."

It did not end there. She texted back, insisting on wanting to meet.

"I want to meet u Sam! I will be waiting for you in front of the Academic block today after class. Please come, for once."

I didn't reply. I was in a dilemma and my fickle mind wasn't able to decide if I should go or leave it. I thought about everything, including our memories.

Finally, I decided that I would meet her. After all, she was my first love. She changed my life. There were sweet and unforgettable moments with her. There was a lot more than nothing, which compelled me to meet her. This time I didn't want to hurt my friends, especially Sanjeet. I asked him about it, showing him the messages. "She has asked me to meet many times before, but this time I want to know what she says. Should I go?"

"Why are you asking me? It's your call, bro!" Sanjeet said. He put his hand on my shoulder and said, "I care about you, man. It was not personal. If you think it is right, go ahead! We will wait for you at Ohm's shop." He said and left. After the last class for the day, I left the building and headed towards the academic block.

Autumn had arrived. Leaves fell off the trees and lay on the road, everywhere. The evening sun's rays slanted directly into one's eyes. The undisciplined wind blew, causing the few leaves that hung onto the trees to detach from their branches and to fly in the air. I walked on Maal Road with the hope of meeting her again. It was a long time since I saw her, and it left me with a tingling sensation within. I had the same sensation I felt in the early days of my friendship with her; I used to run to meet her in high spirits.

I had almost reached, when I saw her standing outside the academic block, waiting for me with eagerness. Her expression changed into a relieved one when she saw me coming towards her. When I reached her, she smiled for a second. I stared at her blankly, recalling the days when I hung out with her all day and she enjoyed herself freely, with me. There always was a notion in her mind that I was there for her all the time. Things had changed now. She had become sincere towards her studies. She was least bothered about her appearance now. This unpretentious and solemn version of Sanjana appeared like Sufiana, to me.

"How are you?" she asked in a whisper.

"I am good." She knew my condition well, anyway.

"Can we talk for some time?" she asked as she came closer.

"Tell me," I said expressionlessly.

Then, out of habit, she held my hand and pulled me to sit on the marble sitting-area on the side of the road. A tear rolled down my cheeks at her sudden action. I remembered our conversations from before. I hid my emotions and let go of her grasp without saying anything. She realized that time and circumstances had changed. She chose to sit in a corner so we could speak peacefully and no one would notice or trouble us. Everybody was familiar with our differences. If they saw us here today, they would get a chance again to make a fuss and it would be annoying for both of us. I was irritated with their inquisitive ways after I stopped talking to and roaming around with her. Her deep black eyes were staring at me as she started speaking. "I know, Sam! I know that I wronged you. I know I have no right to expect forgiveness. But..." She was about to continue, but I interrupted her as my anger came to the fore.

"This is betrayal. You betrayed me, Sanjana. I couldn't have imagined this in my wildest of dreams. I fought with my best friend for you. He always warned me against you, but I listened to you instead of him. I know I am a fool, but you really proved it," I said. She tried to hold my hand to sympathize, but I pulled back with a jerk, showing resentment. A silence hung in the air for a few seconds.

"Did you know that you were the one who showed me real love. You taught me to enjoy and live life," She said.

As the evening wound down, the setting sun's rays filtered through the leaves and fell on her face, making her beauty dazzle. Memories ran in my mind's eye, as I thought of the times when I would steal glances at her, just to enjoy her sheer beauty. I didn't know if I would ever get a chance to admire her from up close, to kiss her intensely and to savor her companionship ever again, with the same ecstatic flavor as we enjoyed before. She continued speaking, "I was trapped before. I fell into the relationship when I was in high school. It was a relationship that fell in line with the fad. He was a smart and tall guy. He proposed to me and I accepted just to show-off that I had a boyfriend! It took a year to understand each other completely. Later, he turned out to be stubborn and possessive. I realized that it wasn't love. I always wanted to live a free life. I chose him to get myself out of the disciplined and restrictive boundaries that my parents set for me. Later on, it happened to be the same thing again. He started restricting me and questioning me for everything."

I listened properly and understood. I knew that she enjoyed her freedom. She was always a free bird. She remained thus in our relationship.

"I didn't want to betray him, either, as he had done a lot for me. No doubt that he loves me, but there is nothing special in that relationship, when compared to your companionship!" she said. I felt somewhat better listening to these praises, but it didn't make any major difference. My suffering and her unfaithfulness was imprinted deeply in my heart.

"I am sorry for what I did to you!" she said genuinely. It aroused my grief. I asked, "Now, you are telling me all these things? Why didn't you tell me the truth before? Why did you keep me in the dark? Whenever I asked you about your past relationships, you ignored me! You manipulated everything, and now you believe that you will create a sad story and get me back?" All my emotions were coming out as anger.

"I have not come here to get you back. I know you won't come back! I just wanted to tell you my story, my feelings and the truth. Just an apology wasn't enough for you. You will always be special in my life. I hope you find somebody who loves you more than you love her! If possible, forgive me," she said and stood up to leave. Tears rolled down her beautiful cheeks, and in a moment, she broke down.

"Listen, Sanjana. At this stage, it is not possible for me to have any relationship with you. It will be annoying for me. I am trying very hard to come out of the nightmare," I said to make her understand my feelings. "I suggest that you try to be true in whatever relationship you are in. Only then you can expect your significant other to be true to you. After that, if it's not working out, do your best to come out of it. Don't hesitate to take necessary steps in life. I know you are like a free bird. You look better when you are free from worries. So, don't compromise with that, otherwise it will choke your real personality!" I said. "It's good to see you studying. I have to start for the next semesters too, as I haven't even seen the syllabus till now!"

I turned to leave, but suddenly, I remembered something and turned around. "Always keep smiling!" She nodded, trying to control her tears. I don't know what made me do it, but instantaneously, I touched her cheek with my right hand. She tried to place her cheek in my palm to feel the touch.

I said goodbye. I couldn't control my tears while coming back, wondering if I should go back and hug her tightly, whisper "I love you" in her ears and kiss her. I controlled myself thinking that she was still in a relationship with that guy; that she betrayed me, that I had to have some loyalty towards my friends, and some respect for myself. With all these thoughts in mind, my self-respect won and I came back, controlling my emotions, without looking back at her.

Chapter Eleven

Reunion

There was exam fever everywhere in college. Practicals were over and theory exams had begun. The first year students were highly worried and tense. It is a universal observation that exam season grips every student, intelligent or dumb. The situation is the same everywhere. All the students become sincere and diligent before exams. It was the same at our college, too. Students could be seen studying all over the place. They were seen struggling day and night at the library, on the terrace of the hostel and sometimes in the rooms of class-toppers, trying to understand the core concepts. This was a time when everybody left other tensions and conflicts aside and earnestly concentrated on getting good grades.

Everyone in our group was in the same spot. Mrinal studied in the library with Rashmi. We had group studies in the hostel, accompanied by frequent rounds of smoking. We were habituated with Mrinal's absence. He was unable to make time for us. We realized that he was highly exhausted with managing his personal affairs and studies. It looked like he was burdened. He was doing all this for his own happiness and love. That was why we couldn't discuss this with him, settling on the assumption that he was almost gone from our group.

Conversely, the friendship was revitalized among us three. Sanjeet, Bhaskar and I enjoyed together through group study. Though we spent more time discussing, planning and gossiping than studying, we managed to face our first exam well. Continuing with the trend, we started preparing for the next exam. After waking up late and having our brunch in the mess, we gathered in Bhaskar's room to study. Bhaskar took out his notes and books from the shelf and occupied his regular spot at the desk. I kept my notes on the bed to start the session. Sanjeet placed a pillow under his arm to have a comfortable posture on the bed while he studied.

"Yaar! Tomorrow is the real test for us. It's going to be the toughest. I am really concerned. S. Bose will have set the paper with his frustration."

"I don't understand why he has issues with all the students!" Bhaskar said.

"Seniors said that he is annoyed with the first year students' behavior and performance. Definitely, he would have set the toughest for us!" I added.

Sanjeet popped up with another concern. "Our cigarette stock is over! There are only two cigarettes left. We need it for the whole day and whole night."

I threw a pillow, showing dissent for his random worry and said, "Leave the cigarette and find a solution for tomorrow's paper, idiot!"

"Why are you so worried? We will do something!" he said as if he could manage easily.

"Then do something!" Bhaskar said.

"See! I have the previous year's papers that I got from the seniors," Sanjeet said. "Secondly, I invited that mugger to teach us some concepts for tomorrow!" Sanjeet nodded towards Nishant.

"At last, we will follow our usual trick! Divide and Rule policy for tomorrow also."

"But you know, Mrinal is the best in this subject. He has got the highest marks in the internals. If he could take out some time for us, it would be a great help!"

"Arey, No worries yaar! We will do well tomorrow!" Sanjeet said.

"Okay then. Let's follow our own practice and start studying." Bhaskar said. He drew his chair towards us to show the division of chapters. We discussed, divided the topics and scheduled a timetable for day and night. The strategic discussion filled me with confidence and we earnestly followed our first session for two hours, with a sutta-break.

"I am going out to buy more sutta. It's over!" Sanjeet said, showing us the empty cigarette packets.

"Leave it Sanjeet! Check if somebody is roaming outside, he can bring it for us," I said. "You should concentrate on studying without wasting time." He seemed unsatisfied. Nevertheless, he called the others to see if somebody had gone out. Bhaskar and I continued studying. After 10-15 minutes, Sanjeet came back saying, "Arey sab ki fati padi hai. No one is out. I think I will go and bring it myself." Bhaskar and I agreed as we were so habituated to smoking that we could not study without a cigarette.

"Okay. Before leaving, check with Mrinal. He is definitely having his educational and romantic session at a restaurant with Rashmi!" Bhaskar said.

"Yes, quite possible," Sanjeet agreed and started calling Mrinal. In a minute he came back saying, "You were right, bro! The idiot is hanging out at Cool Joint with Rashmi. I told him to bring two packs of cigarettes for us. But the only issue is that he will be back after two hours. I think we can manage till then, right?"

"Obviously. Now start studying." Bhaskar said. Sanjeet went back to the bed and resumed studying. Fear for the toughest exam made us study hard. After another rigorous session, Bhaskar started stretching. He looked at the ceiling and said, "Time flies so fast na! We have completed a year in this college."

Our concentration broke. "Yes! We will be seniors next semester! New dumbos will join college and we will rag them!" I said. I was excited at the thought of being the seniors next month onwards.

"Yes! It will be great fun!" Sanjeet said, but it looked like Bhaskar's ideas were going somewhere else.

"Where we will be after college, yaar? Will we be working in MNCs or studying further? We won't be together, right?" Bhaskar went on.

"What are you thinking? Why are you being so pessimistic?" I asked. "I think we will be in touch for a lifetime, bro! It depends on us, how we assimilate our friendship into our lives!"

"Yes! He is right," Sanjeet said.

"I feel like we will be working in the same city, enjoying a good life!" I said optimistically.

"Long drive, discos, weekend parties – It will be full of fun!" I added.

"But no girlfriends, okay?" Sanjeet said, with concern. This made Bhaskar and me laugh out loud.

"You show your machoism everywhere! Bas yahin pe aa ke teri fat jaati hai!" I said and we continued laughing at him.

"As if, you guys have done wonders in the field. You are singles like me!" Sanjeet replied, offended.

"But, our case is not like yours, duffer!" I said. "For me, it was the first time here, but Bhaskar already had a girlfriend in his higher secondary! I don't have to tell you anything about Mrinal, right?" I said.

"Unlike you, we are not hesitant about approaching girls!" Bhaskar said. Sanjeet accepted our win.

"Don't worry, we will give you tips for your married life and tricks to impress your wife," I joked again.

"We know that you are not going to get a girlfriend anyway!" Bhaskar and I laughed and high-fived each other. Sanjeet stood up and jumped on me.

"Saale! You are the only Hrithik Roshan here, hai na?" he taunted as he sat on me and began jumping and hitting me lightly. I was still laughing.

"Yes he is. You are the only Rajpal Yadav here!" Bhaskar could not stop himself and jumped on us. We continued fighting and laughing for a few minutes. The fun diverted us from worrying about the exam. Amidst the fun, Sanjeet's phone rang. He stood up to take the call and Bhaskar and I continued the fun.

"Hey! Shhh..." Sanjeet indicated to us. "Yeah Mrinal! Oh! Rashmi? What happened, Rashmi?" Rashmi had called from Mrinal's phone. "What?" Suddenly he became hyper serious. We stopped our fun and noticed him on call. "We are coming. We are coming!" He said with concern in his voice. There was something wrong with Rashmi or Mrinal and they needed our help. Bhaskar and I looked at each other without a clue, but we were mentally prepared to start. "Don't worry. Everything will be fine. Stay there. We will be there in a minute." Ending the conversation, he gestured with his hand and yelled to us with a tensed demeanour, "Run! Run fast!"

"What happened?" Bhaskar and I asked at the same time. I began wearing my jeans in a hurry. I was in red coloured boxers and couldn't run out wearing that.

"Leave everything and run fast. Those bastards are beating Mrinal outside!" he said. We left the room.

"What? Who?" Bhaskar asked and a sudden apprehension flared on his face. We were running on Maal Road like three Milkha Singhs running for the medal.

"Who else, those locals! I will nail those bastards." Sanjeet said angrily. A sense of precariousness ran in my mind while running, as a picture of Mrinal's bloodied condition and the ugly fight flashed in front of my eyes. I was terrified of fighting and had never been involved in any physical clash before. But, it seemed today, that I had to face it too.

"Hey! Run and tell Sabu Sir that the locals are beating Mrinal at the Dropping Point. Run fast!" Sanjeet said to a classmate who was passing by.

"Okay!" He was startled by Sanjeet's words. Without comprehending anything, he started running towards the seniors' hostel. I realized that the guy was Rohit and that he would surely inform Sabu sir. I was confident about Sanjeet's move. Sabu sir was known for his physique and had a good reputation in the college. Thankfully, Sanjeet had a good rapport with him. In about a minute, we reached the main gate. Without stopping there, Sanjeet said to the security guards, "We will sign the register while entering. It's urgent now." They didn't stop us. Sanjeet was smart. He didn't tell them about the brawl, as it was obvious they would not have helped us outside campus. They would have informed the authorities instead. Instead of helping, the management would take it as a violation of rules and just brazenly punish us. We turned towards the Dropping Point which was not populous in the evening. Because of the local factories in the lane, it had become desolate after dawn. Students used the lane because it was a shortcut to the campus. In half a minute, we reached the point and saw a dreadful scene. Mrinal lay unconscious on the floor with his shirt half-bloodied. His cheek was red and swollen, and looked like he was beaten up badly. Rashmi was terrified and was weeping. She had Mrinal's head on her lap as she tried to wake him. About 12- 15 yards ahead, a handful of locals were running away.

As soon as Rashmi saw us, she broke down. "Please save Mrinal! Please! He is not opening his eyes. Please save him!" She was hardly able to speak. My senses were blocked after seeing all this.

"Bhaskar! Get water and sprinkle it on Mrinal's face. Nothing will happen!" Sanjeet screamed. "Don't worry, Rashmi! Everything will be fine. Those are the bastards, right?" he asked, pointing at the locals. She nodded.

Sanjeet ran after them, screaming, "Hey you Motherfuckers! Cowards! Wait!"

"Sanjeet wait! They are six!" Bhaskar asked him to wait. He left angrily. Everything scared me about the situation. I wasn't sure what to do.

"Sam! Go after him. Try to manage the situation. I will join you soon." Bhaskar said. My blood froze. I began running after Sanjeet. "Oh God! Save me this time," I prayed fervently.

There were six people. Two of them had sticks in hand. Sanjeet seized one of their collars. He had a stick in hand, and Sanjeet pushed him with ferocity. "Show me your manhood, you coward!" he screamed wildly! Sanjeet pushed him and began delivering hard punches to his nose and stomach. The guy's head hit a brick when he fell. He became unconscious. The others started pulling and beating Sanjeet from behind. He smacked one of them down.

Nobody had noticed me approaching, as they were struggling with Sanjeet. They were baffled and infuriated by his appearance and at what had happened to their friend. I picked up a bamboo stick from the roadside and prepared for the fight. The scene had changed in a moment. Three of them held Sanjeet from behind. Before I could do anything, one of them hit him hard on his stomach. Sanjeet bent over in pain. One of them noticed me, but before he could caution the others, I collected my strength and smacked him with the stick. I missed his head and struck his back. It was so hard that he started wiggling and screaming. "Aaaah! My back. I am gone now. Kill that bastard!" As soon as he said it, two of them cornered me. One of them screamed, "You bloody outsider!" and jumped on me. He held me from behind, but at the same time, I hit the other guy with my stick. In this mess, the strike wasn't powerful. They clasped me and snatched the stick from my hand.

"Saale! Bloody loser. You attack from behind, haan? Let me show you how to strike!" One of them turned towards me, folding his sleeves and getting ready to attack me. A sudden wave of terror took over my mind. I was unable to move from their grasp. The third guy was ready to hit me. Sanjeet was struggling with two of them, and Bhaskar was nowhere to be seen. Nobody was around to save me. I closed my eyes and held my breath and realized that I had been given two powerful punches on my stomach. For a moment, I saw stars and the next moment, I screamed in pain.

"What did you do? Coward assholes! Six people ambushed one!" Bhaskar joined us. He pulled a fistful of one of the guy's hair. I was relieved that he had joined in. One of the guys still held me tight. One hit me twice just under my right eye. My face went numb before I felt unbearable pain. Mrinal had also joined in. He pulled the guy who hit me and started hitting him wildly. Mrinal looked tired, but seeing us fight for him may have re-energized him. I was nearly free, but was not in the condition to fight back as my stomach hurt badly, and my right eye swelled up.

With their well-built physiques, Mrinal and Sanjeet fought them hard, though they looked frail with their bruises and injuries. Ignoring my pain, I stood up with ardour and started chasing the guy who ran after assessing that the situation was out of their control. I drew my leather belt from my trousers and started hitting him with the belt while I chased him. I made him run like a dog on the streets. After running a distance of nearly 20 yards, I saw a handful of local senior citizens coming our way. As soon as this guy saw them, he hid behind them and said to them, "These are the bloody outsiders, fighting our people there!"

I stopped in my tracks. My confidence dimmed. The guy who was first smacked by Sanjeet stood with them, with a hockey stick in hand. We didn't know when he had run away from there and called more locals. I thought this was my turn to run away. Without wasting time, I turned around and ran at the same speed I chased him with. They ran behind me, shouting, "Catch him! Wait! You Bastard. Don't let him go."

As soon as I reached my first battleground without getting caught, I saw that Sabu sir and his group had reached and the fight had stopped. I heaved a sigh of relief, assuming that the seniors would handle the situation now. When the locals saw Sabu sir and his group, one of their leaders began speaking. "Arey Sabu! You are also involved! Then it seems that it is an important matter!" It seemed like they knew each other.

"Yes. It is important! It is important when one student is ambushed by six people, that too without considering that a girl is present!" Sabu sir replied in a stern voice. "It is important when you graduates and locals are involved in a junior's matter without knowing the actual story behind the scene!"

"See, Sabu, I respect you. When it comes to injustice to our people, we have to take a stand. We didn't come to fight here!" the senior said in a raised voice.

"I can see that. That's why you guys were chasing a first year kid!" Sabu sir pointed at me. Though he underestimated me, I was proud at his sense of responsibility and helpfulness.

Sabu sir sought to have a private conversation with the leader in private. He agreed. We realised that it was for a negotiation. The fight was over. We sat aside with a sense of relief and pride. Mrinal and Rashmi were still tensed. We were trying to give their mood a boost while also keeping an eye on Mrinal's injuries. Rashmi was overwhelmed by our support. She was sobbing and thanking us reverently. Other seniors who came with Sabu sir joined in to console us and appreciated our courage. Both leaders took around 15 minutes to settle the superfluously hyped matter. They came to Mrinal and Rashmi to confirm the story behind the scenes. Rashmi began to recount the tale of how the local juniors started commenting and teasing her. Mrinal tried to stop them and the fight began. She said that all this had begun when Rashmi had complained about the locals to one of the professors in class for passing comments at her, and they were punished.

The seniors were amazed after listening to the story. They realized that Rashmi and Mrinal were faultless in the whole episode and the juniors involved had lied to them. The matter was settled completely. The juniors were scolded by the seniors and were asked to apologise to Rashmi. Sabu sir asked us and other seniors to vacate the place and move back to the hostel. He specifically instructed Sanjeet to take the injured to the college dispensary. He himself stayed there, perhaps to have a conversation with the locals. I was impressed by his charisma and his way of dealing with complex issues. Everybody admired him for it. Leaving them behind, we left to the college. While entering the main gate, we saw a small crowd of first and second year students and two security guards coming up to us. We realized that news of the incident had spread, and they were coming to help us.

"Where you all are going? You have an exam tomorrow, right?" Sabu sir's best friend, Ankit asked.

"Sir, we heard that there was a fight going on outside with first year students. We thought our guys were in trouble, so we came out!" One of them came up and replied.

"There's nothing to worry. There was some confusion, but everything has settled now. Let's go back to our hostels. Thanks for coming!" Ankit said. Now it was almost certain that disciplinary action would be taken against us as the news was already spread in college.

"What happened Mrinal? And you Sam?" One of our classmates asked, looking at our injuries.

He has been injured. First, we will go to the dispensary. We will speak later! Let's move! Move Guys!" Ankit sir commanded.

We started walking back to the campus. I realized that almost 20 students including us were marching up the steps, discussing the fight. Others treated us with respect after knowing about the actual incident and our courageous efforts. We were filled with pride. It was reflected on our faces. We reached the college dispensary and found that the duty doctor and nurse were around. After examining us and asking us some questions on the incident, the doctor asked others to vacate the place. He began preparing the medicines to dress our wounds. Following his instructions, others left the dispensary. The nurse started dressing my eye. Mrinal was getting a few stitches in his head. He was still in pain and was controlling himself. Rashmi was grimacing as Mrinal felt the pain. With minor injuries, Sanjeet and Bhaskar seemed fine.

After the treatment, we came out and headed towards the hostel. Mrinal had a bandage on his head. Almost all the seniors had left, but some of the batch mates were still accompanying us. We dropped Rashmi at the girls' hostel first. She thanked everyone emotionally before leaving. "I am really sorry guys! I never tried to mix with you. Thank you for what you did today!" she said, with tears in her eyes.

"Hey! That's fine. Mrinal is our bro. We had to come!" Bhaskar consoled her.

"All the best for tomorrow's exam," she said and then moved close to Mrinal. "Take care of yourself!" she said to Mrinal, looking straight into his eyes and touching his cheek affectionately.

"Let's go guys. Let the love birds have their time," I said, and the others, including Rashmi smiled at my comment. "Mrinal! Are you coming back or are you going to make some arrangements in the girl's hostel for tonight?" Bhaskar joked, and we walked towards our hostel. Everybody shared a light laugh. It relaxed us after the terrible incident.

"I am coming in a minute, you assholes!" Mrinal replied with a smile.

He joined us without spending much time. We had to reach our rooms. Others who were still accompanying us left for their rooms to study for the exam. We entered Bhaskar's room in a frazzled condition.

"And, now we have to study whole night. Uff!" I said with exhaustion. We sat down on the bed and some chairs.

"I am very hungry now," Sanjeet said.

"Waise bhi maar khane ke baad bhookh jyada lagti hai!" I said, holding my stomach. We laughed. We were trying to ease our tensions and exhaustion, and to get over the incident. Mrinal was expressionless and still occupied with the whole episode.

"It's 9:40 PM. Dinner will be over in the mess!" I said.

"Leave it, yaar! We will buy some snacks from the cafeteria in the hostel," Bhaskar said.

In a couple of minutes, we settled down without further discussion. The scenes of the clash were running in the back of our minds.

"Saale Sam! How come you showed your heroism today? If you would not have come on time, they would have killed me!" Sanjeet thanked indirectly me as I was checking out my swollen eye in the mirror.

"Arey, leave that. See my eye. Those bastards have hit me like crazy!" I said, showing them my eye. "But, my first shot was good na?" I asked.

"Others should have seen your face while you were getting ready to hit him. It looked like you had constipation and were exerting extreme pressure in the bathroom!" Sanjeet said, imitating my expression. Everyone, including Mrinal had a laugh. Mrinal was gradually trying to get out of his gloom. Suddenly, he turned emotional as he started speaking. "I am sorry Guys! I am sorry that I could not understand the value of friendship. I was not there when you needed me but you always came for me!" It turned into a serious and emotional environment as Mrinal realized his guilt. "Today, you have proved why friendship is as important as any other relationship in our lives! I was lost in my relationship with Rashmi and I didn't realize that I was going away from you all!" he said, making us emotional, too, in the process. "Today, I was helpless. Nobody was there to help when they started teasing me and fighting with me. I had to protect Rashmi anyhow. But, I failed!" A tear trickled and fell off his eye while he was recollecting the incident. "I tried to avoid the fight situation by saying that Rashmi was there and that we could fight later. But those bastards didn't show any respect for the girl!"

"I tried to handle the fight, but they were six people. They didn't show me any mercy. I saw Rashmi crying and pleading with them to leave me!" he couldn't stop crying. Sanjeet and I sat beside him on the bed. Bhaskar sat on the floor by his leg, consoling him.

"Arey! Everything is fine now. Relax! Those things are over. You did the best anyone could do." I patted him.

"You guys are incredible. Despite my distance, you came for me, fought them without thinking for a second that they were locals and more in number!" Mrinal gushed. We were emotional too, as we listened to him speak. "I am a lucky bastard with a loving girlfriend and caring friends who are ready to do anything for me! Thank you God!" Everybody was moved to tears. "I am sorry Bhaskar. I am sorry guys!" Mrinal said, holding Bhaskar's hand.

"It's okay, bro!" Bhaskar said. Our friendship was emotionally revitalized.

"Okay. Enough of sentimental scenes!" Sanjeet said, trying to change the topic. "It's time to celebrate as we are back now! The backbenchers are back with a bang." Sanjeet stood up and yelled out.

"Yes! We are back in business!" Bhaskar said, and we stood up, supporting Sanjeet's enthusiasm. The emotionally charged atmosphere had now lightened.

"We will rock the classroom, the students and the entire college!" Mrinal joined in, passionately. "The fun days are back. Yo!"

"Let's promise ourselves that whatever changes may take place in our lives, whatever problems we may face, we will keep our friendship alive by accompanying and supporting each other!" Sanjeet said, offering his hand to take a promise from everyone.

"Most importantly, we will be committed to having fun all the time!" I said as everyone slapped their hands onto Sanjeet's palm, to make the promise.

After a long time, we realized the importance of true friendship. It filled us with passion and zeal. We couldn't sleep all night, despite having a lot of pain physically. We thoroughly enjoyed studying, gossiping and playing pranks on each other without worrying about the coming disciplinary action against us, and the fear for tomorrow's exam. I was elated at our coming together, and was proud on being an integral part of "The Backbenchers."

Afterword

With our reunion, the fun-filled days were back. It was full of zest and brought back the flavors of happiness in our friendship.

The ultimate rule of nature says "Change is inevitable". Falling under the rule, we couldn't stop some positive and negative vicissitudes in our lives. Some major events changed our lives substantially. The next three years turned into the most unforgettable journey of our lives.

Though our friendship was maintained throughout, the changes we faced in our careers and love-lives, and the story of what happened to Sanjana - will all unfold in the next half of The Backbench Masti-keers. Till then, keep your expectations alive and high!